CHOCOLATE CAKE & WHIPPED CREAM

Edited by

MARCUS ANTHONY

Herndon, VA

ISBN 13: 978-1-61303-076-9

Published in the United States by STARbooks Press

PO Box 711612, Herndon, VA 20171

Many thanks to graphic artist John Nail for the cover design.

Mr. Nail may be reached at: tojonail@bellsouth.net.

Printed in the United States

Herndon, VA

Titles by Marcus Anthony

The Sweeter the Juice

Tall, Dark & Delicious

Spice Men

Black Dungeon Masters

The Color Sexy

Latin Lovers

Chocolate Cake & Whipped Cream

Contents

ONCE YOU'VE HAD BLACK
By Donald Webb

Donald Webb is a published author with two recent novels. He may be reached at: andon402@shaw.ca

Trent was leaving a gay bar, when he noticed Kyle, a student from his college, strolling down the sidewalk. Trent was surprised to see him in the mainly gay section of the city. Two weeks before, Trent and a couple of his buddies were sitting on the grass in the college quad when Kyle, a college basketball player, and another jock walked past them. Kyle had sneered at them, and his jock friend had said, "Faggots." And yet here he was, hanging out in "Faggot Land." When Kyle walked into a bar, well-known for its dungeon, Trent decided to follow him. Maybe I'll find a way to get back at the phony homophobe Trent was thinking as he entered the bar.

The bar was packed with hot hunks. Trent purchased a beer and then leaned against the bar, so he could keep an eye on Kyle. It's a pity the sexy stud's such a bigot Trent was thinking, because he's gorgeous. Trent had been attracted to the six-foot-six black stud ever since he'd first seen him dashing around the basketball court.

Kyle finished his beer and moved away from the bar toward a door in the far end of the room. When Kyle descended the stairs into the dark dungeon, Trent was right behind him. There were only a few dim red lights, spread around the room, so it took Trent a few moments to get his bearings. Guys were having sex right out in the open, some on low bunk beds, and others standing up.

He followed Kyle through a steel door into an old meat freezer. Kyle pushed his way through the crush of bodies and moved into an even darker area of the freezer. If Trent hadn't stuck to Kyle, he would never have been able to find him. They squeezed into a tight corner with bodies packed around them.

At first, Trent felt panicked at the crush of sweaty masculine bodies. It brought back the claustrophobic fear he'd suffered as a child. He made an effort to get his breathing under control, forced himself to relax, and slowly responded to the erotic sensations of anonymous men groping him.

When hands rubbed his ass cheeks and basket, he did the same to Kyle. He often dreamed about being gangbanged by the mainly black basketball team, so to him, this was a dream come true. He'd never had sex with a black stud, but he'd always wanted to try it. He'd heard the old saying, "Once you've had black, you'll never go back," so he wanted to see if it were true. His one hand slowly stroked Kyle's hard boner through his tight jeans while his other hand massaged Kyle's rear-end. Kyle, who was himself busy with the other bodies pressed against him, ignoring Trent. Someone undid Trent's jeans and pushed them and his briefs down his thighs. Trent did the same to Kyle and then held Kyle's hard shaft when it sprang into the open.

Fuck! It's true, Trent thought as he stroked Kyle's massive dick. I wouldn't mind him throwing it into me. He ran his thumb over the slick meatus and slid his fist down the long shaft to Kyle's pendulous nuts. His other hand rubbed the mounds of Kyle's muscular ass then his fingers probed the moist hairy crevice. Trent turned Kyle around, and then bent over to taste Kyle's dick. He let his tongue dig into the slit of Kyle's dick-head then he mouthed the crown and slowly sank it deep into his throat. Even in the darkened busy space, he could hear Kyle let out a groan, and say, "Suck that dick, bro."

As Trent sucked Kyle, someone knelt before Trent and sucked Trent's dick. His hard shaft sank down the pliable throat, all the way to his balls. He was enjoying the excellent blowjob, when he felt a strong pair of hands spread his ass-cheeks and a moist tongue on the entrance to his chute. Trent could feel another tongue on Kyle's shaft. He could just make out the handsome features of the young man sharing Kyle's boner. When Trent's lips came to the head of Kyle's shaft, the young guy kissed Trent, and then together, they mouthed Kyle's bloated dickhead. The young guy claimed possession of the basketball player's joint and deep-throated him as Trent licked his nuts. Trent could feel someone licking between Kyle's asscheeks, so he slowly straightened up and abandoned Kyle's ass and dick to the aggressive guys on their knees.

Kyle held onto Trent for support. His hand wrapped around Trent's dick. "Oh yeah," he groaned, "nice and thick ... just how I like them." Is this the same guy, flashed through Trent's mind, as he stared into Kyle's face? It is, he decided. Next Kyle pulled Trent's mouth to his and sucked Trent's tongue.

Trent whispered in Kyle's ear, "Turn around, I want to taste your butt."

Kyle did as requested and pressed his back against Trent's body. Trent sank to his knees and pushed his nose into the valley between Kyle's ass cheeks. God, he thought, his butch ass smells better than any ass I've ever smelled. I wonder if he's ever been fucked? He sniffed for a while, and then he spread the muscular mounds and licked the moist, hairy, crevice. When his tongue zeroed in on Kyle's tight hole, Kyle bent forward and, using his hands, spread his cheeks wide apart. He pushed his butt against Trent's face and moaned. "Oh yeah ... eat that ass, bro. Show me how much you like that black ass."

Trent kept licking and probing the tight slit, until Kyle relaxed enough for his tongue to slip all the way in. He licked his middle finger and gently pushed it into Kyle's hot chute. He finger fucked Kyle for a short while, and then tried to insert a second finger, but Kyle was too tight. Trent pulled a tube of lube out of his pocket, spread the viscous substance over two of his fingers, and then he resumed his assault on Kyle's butt hole. This time his fingers slipped all the way in. His own butt was craving cock, so he applied lube to his other hand and fingered his own asshole.

Kyle's but quivered around Trent's probing fingers. "Fuck, that feels good," he said as he pushed back hard against Trent's palm.

Trent applied more lube to his fingers and managed to get a third one into Kyle's tight chute. He twirled his fingers around and around, until Kyle's hole felt completely relaxed, then he dug deeply, until four of his fingertips were massaging Kyle's hard gland.

Kyle reached between his legs and stroked Trent's boner. "Fuck me," he said.

Trent stood up and placed the head of his dick next to his fingers, and then slowly replaced his fingers with his boner. He shoved into Kyle's hot chute – still not believing it was happening, until he was fully embedded in Kyle's silky smooth channel. He placed his arms around Kyle and pulled him against his body. "Nice hot hole, dude," he said.

Kyle pushed a hand between his legs and felt his hole. "Oh yeah," he gasped, "pound me with that big dick."

Trent started a slow back and forth movement. "Feels good, doesn't it?" he whispered in Kyle's ear.

Kyle turned his face toward Trent. "Fuck yeah ... I've needed a good fucking for a long time."

Trent placed his lips on Kyle's lips. Kyle opened his mouth wide and sucked Trent's tongue. They kissed for a while, and then Trent picked up speed and began long poling Kyle. "Fuck me, bro. Fuck me with that big white cock," Kyle bellowed as he leaned over and spread his butt cheeks. It's only because of the anonymity of the situation, Trent thought, that's why he's so brazen. Tomorrow he'll be back to his old macho behavior.

Ah, good, Trent thought when he felt a couple of fingers sliding into his own chute. He stopped pounding Kyle, spread his own cheeks, pushed back on the fingers, and then groaned when the fingers probed deep into his channel. "Fuck me, dude," he moaned when the fingers were replaced by a hard knob. "That's it, dude," he said over his shoulder, "give it to me." He moved his hand and placed his fingers around the huge slab of meat when it started slipping in and out of his chute. When he felt the pubes of the guy fucking him, he knew his dream had come true. He was sandwiched between two huge black guys.

Kyle placed his hands on Trent's ass and pulled him into him. "Fuck me, bro," he groaned. "Stop messing around ... pound me with that big dick."

Trent picked up speed, banging his butt against the hips behind him, and plowing Kyle's muscular rear-end. The guy's huge knob, deep inside his chute, was playing havoc with his prostate. He couldn't hold back any longer. "I'm coming, dude," he whispered in Kyle's ear. "I'm shooting up your butch basketball butt."

When Trent's chute clamped down on the dick up his ass, the guy behind him groaned, "Coming, dude ... coming in your white ass."

"Yeah ... yeah," Kyle said as his ass milked Trent's dick and his load erupted into a cocksucker's mouth. "Take my load."

When the guy behind Trent pulled his dick out of Trent's slimy hole, someone else tried to get in. Trent pushed him away and pulled Kyle with him as he backed against a wall. Trent and Kyle kissed for a long moment. Kyle gasped when Trent's cock slipped from his well-fucked hole. Trent turned Kyle around, pulled him against his chest, and held the gasping jock's asscheeks in his hands. His fingers played with Kent's oozing hole, as cum dripped from his own hole.

Trent was amazed to feel a hard cock slipping between his fingers into the hole he had just vacated. The cock was balls deep by the time Kyle realized what was happening. He squirmed around in Trent's arms. "Oh good," he said as the cock started pounding, "Just what I need!"

"Feels good, doesn't it," Trent said when Kyle wiggled his butch ass. "Yeah," Kyle said. "I gotta admit, bro, it does."

They kissed as Trent held Kyle's ass-cheeks tightly in his hands, keeping them spread apart to assist the fucker. It didn't take long for the guy fucking Kyle to unload. He grunted loudly as he shot his load up the basketball player's ass. Trent felt the creamy shaft slip through his fingers when the guy pulled it from Kyle's ravished butt hole. Before the guy's stalk was completely out of Kyle's hole, there was another hard cock waiting to replace it. Oh, good, Trent was thinking, they're lining up to fuck the homophobic jock's chute. I'll have to remind him about it tomorrow when I see him in the quad.

Kyle, seeming to be totally out of control, groaned, "Oh yeah, fuck my ass."

Trent was amazed at the change in Kyle's demeanor. It seemed he'd suddenly morphed from an uptight homophobic jock, to an in-heat

5

bitch. Kyle called out, "Oh, yeah, ream that hole. I need to be fucked good. Gimme more."

And more he got. Trent had his hands around the entrance to Kyle's hole, so he could feel the huge cock pistoning in and out of Kyle's chute. Kyle rested his head on Trent's shoulder. Trent physically supported him, while Kyle got his ass used, and abused, by the pack of hungry men. Trent lost count of the actual number and was astounded at the amount of cum oozing from of Kyle's asshole.

He decided he'd had enough. It was time to go. When he whispered in Kyle's ear, "Good fuck, Kyle. See you on campus." A shocked look appeared on Kyle's face. Trent extricated himself from the pack, pulled up his jeans, and forced his way through the crush of bodies. He breathed a sigh of relief when his sweaty body was eventually outside in the cool fresh air. On the way home, he thought about Kyle. He's probably wondering who it was that fucked him, and how come I knew his name. I'll speak to him on Monday. I'll go easy on him. It's true what they say. I'll never go back!

BEEFCAKE BIRTHDAY CAKE
By Logan Zachary

Logan Zachary (LoganZachary2002@yahoo.com or www.loganzacharydicklit.com) lives in Minneapolis, MN. He has a new book and more than 100 stories in various anthologies.

My birthday was coming in two days, and true to form, my partner, Jake, wasn't able to come up with a cake. I asked for a simple Dairy Queen ice cream cake. Nothing fancy, nothing elaborate. Just a plain old ice cream cake. How simple could that be?

"I'm not buying you a stupid ice cream cake, Tyler. You're thirty-two. You're not getting a Dairy Queen cake. Those are for kids. You're an adult. You need a real birthday cake. So what would you like?"

"I told you, I just want a simple Dairy Queen cake. Can't I be a kid for one more year?" My blond hair fell into my eyes, and I pushed it behind my ear. It was time for a long overdue haircut.

For some reason Jake had his own idea of what was right for me. In other words, what Jake wanted was right, and what I wanted didn't matter. He was always in control. His clothes never wrinkled; he never spilled food on his shirt; even his dark brown hair stayed perfectly in place as mine had a mind of its own.

"Wouldn't you like a nice cheesecake, or how about a rich chocolate cake, maybe a raspberry torte? Anything you want." His chiseled body looked as if he never ate sweets and worked out twenty-four-seven.

Anything, except a Dairy Queen ice cream cake, I thought. "Okay, what would you want me to want?" My body was solid, but my muscles were smooth and toned, not ripped like his, maybe the Dairy Queen did hold me back a little, but I was happy.

Jake rolled his eyes. "Come on, let's go to the bakery, and see what they have."

Icing on the Lake overlooked Lake Superior in Duluth, Minnesota, and they always had the best buns, breads, and pastries. Zack Connor was the new owner. He also had nice buns, and a trimmed black beard, furry chest and muscular arms. I know because I always enjoyed coming to his bakery for lunch on Saturdays after shopping in the stores along Superior Street.

"Will I get a gift card for We're Wolfe's Books this year? Will I, huh will I?" I loved horror movies and scary books, both were the best gifts possible, but Jake hated giving them to me. He never knew what to buy and didn't respect the genre, so he gave sexy underwear and porn, practical gifts.

"You're such a child." Jake pulled into a parking spot next to the front door of Icing on the Lake.

"Isn't that a good thing?" I asked, as I unbuckled my seatbelt.

Jake turned and kissed me. "You're a good thing, just difficult to live with at times."

"At times?"

"All the time." He opened his car door and waited for me as we walked to the bakery's entrance. The sweet smell of freshly baked bread filled the cool fall air.

"How do people live and work around here and not weight three hundred pounds."

"Will power," Jake said. He turned his back to me and headed to the door. His tight ass was hugged perfectly in his tight faded jeans; the seam rode deep into his crack. Beautiful.

I wondered if that was an insult to me? But after such a wonderful sight, I let it slide. "I thought Zack had today off."

"He does, but he hired a new baker and a cake expert, so I hope he'll be able to make the perfect cake for my man."

"Why all of this sweet talk? What are you up to?" I asked suspiciously.

"You worry too much."

"I have met you, and I know you well."

Jake held the door open for me and slapped my butt as I entered the bakery.

As we headed through the dining area to the display cases, a handsome black man stepped out of the kitchen wiping his hands on a towel. "Good afternoon, and welcome to Icing on the Lake." The man's smile brightened when he saw Jake. "Hey, Jake, is this your partner? He's way too good for you."

This man was handsome, smart, and had great taste. I liked him immediately. He was dark brown, bald, beefy, and built. His muscles had muscles, but how did Jake know him? From the gym? I turned to look at him, and he saw my expression.

"Tyler, honey, this is Shawn. He was my old roommate in college. He called and was looking for a job in Duluth, and I put him in contact with Zack."

Zack wasn't working today, but his hunky assistant sure was. I looked deep into his dark brown eyes. Shawn looked more like a linebacker than a baker, but after seeing the display case filled with amazing treats; his skills in the delicate designs of cakes were amazing.

"Shawn won't admit it, but rumor has it that he was on one of those upper channel networks on a cake decorating show," Jake said.

"I don't know anything about that." Shawn pursed his lips and turned to me. "So, how can I help you guys today?" he asked.

"Tyler's birthday is coming up, and I want to get him a cake." Jake leaned over the display case to look at the goodies.

Shawn turned to me and asked, "What kind of cake do you want?"

"I love the Dairy Queen ice cream cakes."

Jake poked me in the back, as Shawn said, "That's a fun cake."

"But I was told I'm too old for that cake."

Shawn looked at Jake and smiled. "I can see you're as subtle as always." He scratched his head and asked, "Do you like chocolate?" He strutted his cocoa physique as he asked.

I scanned his whole body, from tip to toe. He even flipped up his apron and turned around to show me his booty.

"Shawn," Jake's voice took on a warning tone.

"Can't a brother have a little fun? Lighten up." He turned back to me. "Do you want nuts or no nuts? Hot, rich, and gooey on the inside, or long, hard, and tall on the outside?" His facial expressions showed raw sexuality.

I had to be careful how I answered this question. "What kind of cake would you make for Jake?"

"Jake's cake?" Shawn smiled. "He told you that story?"

Jake's face burned red.

"Oh, I guess not. He didn't tell you. Naughty boy, you're such a sheet." Shawn scolded and swore as he waved a finger at him.

I turned to Jake and asked, "What's this about Jake's cake?"

Jake knew he was busted, and he wished the ground would swallow him whole. "Maybe a Dairy Queen ice cream cake isn't such a bad idea."

"Oh no, Dear. For my birthday, I want a Jake cake, no matter how fattening it is, or how unhealthy it is."

Shawn laughed as he looked at Jake and waited for the explosion.

None came.

I was even surprised.

"So is it okay if I make him a Jake cake?" Shawn asked.

I had never seen him so defeated. What was wrong? Okay, I'll let him off the hook and play nice. "Why don't you make me a Black Forest cake and call that good?"

Jake cringed at what I said, and Shawn just nodded. "A Black Forest cake it is."

"Shawn, I hope you can come to our house tomorrow night for my birthday supper, drinks, and cake." I invited him to our party.

Shawn looked into Jake's eyes and waited.

"Yes, Shawn, I'd love to see you again, and I'd love for you to get to know Tyler, better. Please come over." Jake pulled out a business card and handed it to Shawn. "Join us for drinks at six, dinner is at seven, and hopefully dessert will be at eight."

"Sounds like fun." Shawn pulled out a business card of his own and handed it to me. "Call me if you want to change the cake," he held up his large hand to cover his mouth, "he doesn't have to know."

"Thanks," I said, as Jake pulled me out of Icing on the Lake. At the car, I pulled my arm free of his grasp, twisting it too hard, and I rubbed it where it hurt. "I'm sorry about that."

Jake walked around the car and unlocked the doors.

As I got in and buckled my seatbelt, I said, "We can skip that cake if that is going to be an issue." I reached over to touch his hand.

He tried to pull away, but I held onto him.

"Talk to me. Were you and Shawn …" I left the sentence finish itself.

Jake swallowed hard. "He was my old roommate in college, and he was an old lover." He stared straight ahead and avoided my gaze.

"Do you want to get back together with him? He sure is sexy. I could see why you would want to get back with him."

"I love you." Jake turned to me.

"I know, but that doesn't mean he still isn't exciting to you. He got my blood pumping, and he's a nice guy. Who wouldn't like him?" Then I paused. "Is that why he moved to Duluth?"

Silence.

I squeezed his hand. "Is it?"

"No. He's a great friend, sexy as sin, but I love you, and I only want you."

"But he moved to Duluth. If this cake is …"

"It's fine." He turned to me. "I just wanted your day to be special."

"My birthday will be perfect as long as you're there."

Jake leaned forward and kissed me. Then we headed off to home.

# # # # #

My birthday was perfect. It dawned sunny and warm for a fall day. As I rolled over in bed, I stretched my arms over my head. It felt so good for my back.

Jake rolled over on top of me, naked and wide awake. His hands traced up along my arms and tickled the hair in my pits as he leaned down to kiss me. "Good morning, birthday boy."

My hands held onto the bars of the headboard as his tongue entered my mouth.

His hands worked higher up my arms, and I didn't know what he was doing until I heard the metallic click of the handcuffs.

I opened my eyes and looked into his baby blues.

He smiled as he continued to kiss me. "Happy Birthday," he said as he broke our kiss. He licked over to one arm pit and made my whole body tingle.

"Stop that, it tickles." I tried to pull away, but my arms were held firmly in place, wide open.

He licked over to a nipple and swirled around it before kissing it. After it rose to a point, he drew it into his mouth and rolled the aroused end between his teeth. He bit down gently on it.

"Stop."

He pinched my other one before tickling my other armpit.

I could smell the sweat from my body.

Jake had showered already and smelled fresh of soap and water. I loved a clean body; he enjoyed a sweaty, manly musk. He pushed his still damp, hairy body down my torso, his bare butt rolled over my erection. His fingers trailed down my sides, the most sensitive places on my body.

I was extremely ticklish along the cum-gutters, those deep lines along my torso, which so many hot men had, perfect for come to roll off their bellies and run down their legs.

He licked down my abs and entered my hairy belly button. His teeth pulled on the hair there and sent pre-cum oozing out of my cock. His razor stubble brushed against the fat mushroom head of my engorged cock and sent sharp scratches over the tender skin. He was such a tease.

He rose up and after cleaning the pre-cum from my tip, he licked down my shaft to my full balls. He tongued a ball before pulling it into his mouth. He tried to swallow the heavy orb.

I pushed my hips into his face, force feeding him my sac.

He took it and sucked my other ball into his mouth.

"Ah," I moaned.

13

"Did you want a birthday blow job?" Jake asked as he let my balls fall out of his mouth. He licked slowly up my shaft and paused at the tip. He ran his hand along the thickness and milked out more pre-cum. He watched as it ran down the underside of my dick. As it passed the ring, he caught it and swallowed with a smile. "Delicious."

I arched my back, begging for more.

His hands grabbed my ass and squeezed, then he spread my cheeks, and his fingers dug into my crease, exploring, seeking a tender opening.

"Yes, yes," I said.

"Maybe I need to taste you." He tipped my pelvis and opened my bottom for his tongue. He looked down and saw the pink spot and kissed it. His nose nuzzled my balls, as his tongue slipped between his lips and sought entry. He curled his tongue for easier entry, but then he opened it wide to lick over the whole hairy hole.

My balls almost lost their load then and there. How I loved his talented tongue. I pulled on the handcuffs, wishing my hands were free to touch him, to caress him, to stroke his beautiful cock and squeeze those low hanging balls.

"Let me do all the work, it's your day, lay back and enjoy." He dove back between my legs and darted his tongue deeper into me.

My cock waved frantically back and forth. "Touch me, touch me," it screamed in my mind.

Jake reached up with one hand and touched him, slowly stroking, squeezing, and sliding to the throbbing tip. He swallowed me again.

"I want to taste you, too. I want you in my mouth," I begged. Then I got images of Shawn and Jake, black and white naked bodies rolling over each other in the bed. My erection grew thicker and longer as I saw myself between these two hot men.

Jake slowly withdrew my cock from his mouth. He crawled off of me and did a one-eighty. He lifted his muscular leg and straddled my face. His hairy hole and balls loomed over my face.

His ass was so perfectly pink; my eyes teared from the sight. Round, perfect, muscular and squeaky clean. What would it look with Shawn's big cock pounding his pucker?

He slipped his dick into my mouth, and I hungrily swallowed him.

I loved the taste of his cock, his balls, of him. He was my man. I loved everything about him.

Jake pulled out of my mouth and slid down my body. "It's your birthday, and I want to suck on you, give you a blow job."

"Maybe I want your cock deep inside me." I grinned at him and brought my butt up and spread my legs wider, tempting him with my ass.

"Do me," I begged.

"Don't you want me? My ass?" Jake asked.

"I do, but I want you in me as you kiss me. I love how you kiss, and I want to know you're there."

Jake slapped his ass. "You don't want to tap this?"

"I want it all, but right now ..."

And he lubed his cock and slammed it into me. His hand worked my cock as he humped my rump. Bamm, bamm, he entered me. He knew where to hit.

"Slow down, I'm close."

Jake's lips came down on my mouth and kissed me. His tongue slipped into my mouth and tasted my tongue. He continued to jack my dick as he pounded my butt. His dick filled my hole and drove the excitement higher.

I couldn't take much more, my balls were about to burst.

He kissed me again, and my balls let loose. Cum flowed out of my cock through his fingers and over my stomach.

Jake gasped, thrust into me, and held me pinned to the headboard. He came in my ass. Hot, white cum filled me, and as he pulled in and out the cream poured out of me and onto the sheets.

I couldn't stop kissing him as he came again inside me, driving another wave of semen out of me.

We lay together as our bodies relaxed. Jake got up and walked to the bathroom.

I heard him pee, and then he returned with a smile.

"Are you going to unlock me?" I waved my hands and made the handcuffs rattle.

He climbed on top of me, straddling my pelvis, and he stroked my cock back to a full erection. He guided his butt over my hard-on. "Round two, birthday boy."

# # # # #

The rest of the day passed by quickly, and before we knew it, it was six. Shawn arrived with a big cake box and a paper bag with handles slung over his forearm. "What a great place you have here."

I ushered him into the kitchen, and he set his supplies down.

"Are you all settled in town yet?" Jake asked as he handed him a glass of wine.

"I'm living at a hotel until I can find a place to live." He looked around the kitchen and beamed.

"Let me show you the house," and Jake took him on a tour of our home.

I wanted to peek at the cake, but I figured it was supposed to be a surprise, so I waited. I poured myself another glass of wine and went to sit in the living room by the fire. The wood crackled as it burned, and the wonderful smell of wood smoke hung in the air. The heat filled the space and made the room cheery and welcoming.

Jake returned with Shawn and let him sit as he went to check on supper. "You have a great place here and thank you for inviting me to the party."

"Actually, we three are the whole party."

Shawn sat forward. "Oh really?"

"I wanted to get to know you better, and this is the best way to do it."

Jake returned with the bottle of wine and refilled our glasses. "Supper will be ready in fifteen minutes." He sat down next to me and placed his hand on my knee.

"How long have you guys been together?" Shawn asked.

"Five years," Jake said, and clicked our wine glasses together.

Shawn held his glass up and toasted us. "How did you guys meet?" he asked me.

"I was picking up a Dairy Queen Birthday cake for a friend's birthday and Speed Racer here comes flying into the parking lot and almost runs me over. Needless to say, the cake was toast."

"I said I was sorry, and I even was a gentleman because I offered to buy you a new one." Jake said as he caressed up my arm. "As we were checking out, I looked into his eyes and then next thing he knew, he had missed the party, the cake was melted and ..."

"Was he always that easy to get into bed?" I asked.

Shawn almost choked on his wine. "Jake was a very uptight virgin. I knew he was gay and wanted me, before he did, but he was so timid."

"Timid? He practically ripped my clothes off in the Dairy Queen's parking lot," I said.

"I can see why," Shawn smiled. "If it wasn't for him sleeping on the top bunk, we would never have had sex. I pulled his underwear off as he tried to crawl into bed. As he hung there, I made him rise to the occasion."

"I can see you doing that very easily," I said, as I adjusted myself in my pants.

Shawn noticed and nodded.

"So what happened?" I asked.

Jake stopped caressing my arm and just held it.

"Graduation came, and we both went home. We tried to make it work, but both of us found jobs in our fields so far apart; we couldn't make it work, so ..."

"We moved on with our lives." Jake stood up. "I think supper is done, come into the dining room in ten minutes."And he left.

Shawn stood up and looked as if he was going to leave.

I patted the spot Jake left.

Shawn walked over with his wine and sat down next to me.

I spread my legs so one touched his leg. I set my glass down and turned to him. Reaching out, I took his head into my hands and looked deep into his eyes. "Jake is an amazing man, and so are you. I can feel that."

Shawn swallowed hard.

I leaned forward and kissed him. His full lips met mine and opened as my tongue explored.

He blindly set his glass down and pulled me closer, adding fire to the kiss.

And he was a great kisser. My head swam as we broke it. "WOW!"

Shawn smiled. "It takes two to make that happen."

"What about three?" popped out of my mouth before I knew what I was saying. My face burned and we stood. "Maybe we should go help."

Shawn grabbed my hand and stopped me. "Jake would never cheat on you, and I respect your relationship. I would never get between you guys."

"Unless we asked," I said.

Shawn was speechless.

"Jake and I have never played around, but for some reason I feel very comfortable with you, as if I have always known you." My cock was rock hard. I glanced down at his groin and saw a straining bulge there, too. I wanted to rub it, but now was not the time.

Shawn turned to head to the dining room, and I slapped his booty. He shook it for me and pushed it back at me to hit it again.

I played the bongos on his butt as we walked to the dining room.

Jake had the table set better than Martha Stewart. She could take lessons from him. He entered the dining room with creamy mashed potatoes and set them down with the perfectly roasted turkey breast, flash fried green beans, stuffing, and cranberries. Candles were lit, and each setting had the fine bone china, champagne flutes and our best silver. "Sit down, and we can get started."

Supper and champagne flowed easily. Everything was delicious, and the conversion was light and entertaining. Our plates were clean, and it was time for dessert.

Shawn pushed himself up from the table and headed into the kitchen.

"You've never told me about the Jake Cake," I said.

Jake's face turned beat red.

"I guess there's a story there." I sat back and smiled. "I like Shawn, a lot. He's very sweet and so sexy. I can see why he's so special to you, and I'm not jealous. Well, I am jealous that I haven't seen him naked …"

Jake spat his champagne across the table.

"Were you thinking the same thing?" I leaned forward on the table and picked up my flute. I raised it to him and drained my glass.

The dining room door opened and a beautiful Black Forest Cake came through the door and Shawn behind it. He approached the table and set it down in front of me.

"I have to tell him," Jake said, instead of singing Happy Birthday.

Shawn sat down and looked at him.

"It was my birthday, and no one was around. So Shawn felt sorry for me and made me a Black Forest Cake, but he modified it a little."

"Do tell," I said, leaning forward.

Jake flushed and couldn't continue.

Shawn turned to me. "Do you want me to show you?" There was a twinkle in his eye and a sly smile on his beautiful mouth.

"Yes."

He picked up the cake and left the room.

I looked at Jake, and he opened his mouth to say something but didn't.

"Okay, I'm not slow. Is he doing something naughty with my cake?"

Jake flushed even a darker red. He bolted to the kitchen door, but I stopped him.

"This is my birthday, all of it. And I want all of it." I wrapped my arms around him and held him close. "I love you." I kissed him and pulled him over to my chair. "Sit on my lap."

"I ..."

"Just do it."

Shawn called from the kitchen. "Ready?"

"Yes," I called.

"No," Jake said.

I slapped him as the door opened up. Candles were added to the cake, each one was sitting in a glop of whipped cream, but one stuck out at a funny angle and had a bigger blob of whipped cream.

Then I noticed how close the cake was to Shawn, how the cake was touching Shawn and Shawn was in the cake, well, part of him was in, a big part.

Shawn started to sing. "Happy Birthday to you." The awkward candle quivered in the cake.

Jake pushed his face into my neck.

I rubbed his back as the cake came closer. "Are you going to help me blow out the candles?" I whispered in his ear.

His whole body tensed.

"Happy Birthday to you," Shawn continued.

"It's okay. I like him, and I want him and you as my perfect birthday present."

The cake was inches from my face, and the whipped cream was starting to run off of the one candle and the head of Shawn's penis was emerging with a candle stuck in the opening. It shook even more as a clear fluid oozed around its base. "Happy Birthday to you, dear Tyler."

"I don't want to blow too hard or your pubes may catch on fire."

"Happy Birthday to you."

I blew as fast as I could, aiming for the one in his dick first and then around the top of the eight-inch cake. Then I realized how big he was. It was going to be a great party.

Jake jumped up and brought the dessert plates over. He also picked up the big knife.

Shawn stepped back from the table.

21

"Stop." I took the candle from his dick and brought it to my mouth, cleaning the whipped cream and Shawn's pre-cum from it. "Delicious." I set the candle on my dinner plate and slowly removed the cake from his cock. I handed the platter to Jake and dropped to my knees. "Let me clean up the pedestal." I licked along his hard dick and watched it wave up and down. My hand couldn't get around its girth as I brought the rich chocolate to my mouth. Cherry juice and whip cream mixed along his shaft as I licked the sweetness into my mouth.

Once clean, I drew him into my mouth.

Jake came to stand next to me with the knife.

I set the knife on the table and pulled Jake to his knees to help lick Shawn's dick.

Our tongues met and together we cleaned the rest of it.

Shawn's pants fell to the floor, and he stepped out of them, giving us access to his huge low hanging balls.

I brought Shawn's fat head to my mouth and licked into his opening before swallowing him as far as I could get.

Jake worked between his legs and sucked on his balls.

My hand reached behind to caress his booty, and it met Jake's as we neared the crease. Our hands intertwined and held there for a few seconds and together spread his cheeks and explored deeper, he felt warm and willing.

Shawn moaned from our attention and let his head fall back as we licked, sucked, and explored. His hand guided my head on his cock, sliding it in deeper.

My finger found his tight pucker and teased it.

Shawn's legs threatened to buckle as I explored. "It's Tyler's birthday, shouldn't he be the center of attention?" Shawn guided my head off his cock and pulled me to my feet. He kissed me deeply, as he blindly reached down for Jake. He pulled him to his feet and made him join into the three-way kiss. All of our tongues rolling around each others'.

My hand cupped his ass, and I kneaded his glutes as we kissed.

Jake finally broke the spell. "Why don't we go upstairs to the bedroom, before dessert?"

"I thought this was dessert." I smiled at the men.

"We'll have several courses of dessert," Jake said. He grabbed the champagne bottle and headed up the staircase.

Shawn followed, and I watched Shawn's amazing bare ass sway up the stairs. How I wanted to bury my face between those chocolate cheeks. Being a bodybuilder, his body was smooth, and his skin looked so soft it glowed.

I reached up and caressed his booty as we walked up the steps. He pushed back on my hand and allowed me to feel the power in his muscles.

Jake pulled the covers back – the sheets were changed and clean from this morning. Lube and condoms were placed on the table, as he pulled his shirt over his head.

Shawn pulled his shirt off and turned to me naked to help me strip. His huge fingers worked nimbly on the buttons and zipper. Before I knew it, I stood wearing only my bulging Calvins. He motioned for Jake to be the one to take off my briefs.

I crawled on the bed and lay in the middle, as the two men joined me on each side. Jake pulled my underwear off, and my cock slapped my belly.

Shawn waited for Jake's okay before swallowing my cock. He swallowed me whole, deep throating me. He closed his mouth and formed a perfect seal on my dick; I thought I was going to come right then. He grabbed my balls and pulled down on them.

Jake kissed me.

"Thank you for the perfect birthday."

"You haven't seen anything yet," Jake said as he pulled one of my legs up.

23

Shawn pulled my other one up and spread me wide open. He moved between my legs and licked between my cheeks. "You're so delicious and tasty." His tongue drilled into my opening as he started to loosen me up.

Jake continued to kiss me. His hands massaged my chest. Never had I been the center of so much attention.

Shawn's head came up from between my legs and smiled at Jake. "He's all loose for you." He started to move out.

"I want to see you pleasure him," Jake said.

I looked down at Shawn's throbbing cock. Could I even take a cock that thick and big inside me?

Jake handed him a condom, but Shawn nodded for him to put it on him. Thrusting his hips forward, Jake was able to apply the condom easier. He used both hands to roll the rubber down his thick shaft. He cupped his balls a few times and squeezed, he drew Shawn to him and kissed him over my pelvis.

I stroked myself several times as I watched them kiss and grope each other. My butt tingled as I thought about the excitement of him plugging my hole.

Jake poured some lube onto Shawn's cock and stroked it, smoothing the lube all over. He motioned down to me and grabbed one of my ankles.

Shawn picked up my ass and guided his dick between my cheeks. He pressed the tip to my opening and held firmly there.

Jake straddled my face with his butt, as he reached down and started to lube up my dick.

My tongue circled Jake's hairy hole.

Shawn leaned forward and kissed Jake as he grabbed his dick. He pulled on his cock, making his balls bounce on my chin.

My tongue entered Jake, and he rocked his hips over my mouth.

Shawn pushed harder against my ass, as Jake jacked my cock. Together, the stimulation helped relax me, and he slowly started to enter me. His tip popped through the tight opening. He rocked back and forth, slowly, inching his way in.

It hurt as he stretched me wider and wider, but my tongue dug deeper into Jake.

Jake worked my cock faster and harder, relaxing me even more and making the pain turn into pleasure.

I could feel him filling me, adding more excitement and stimulation to my body.

Jake's balls started to pull up, so I knew he was getting close.

Shawn rocked his hips again and another inch slid into me. I doubted he would fit all the way inside me, but he was trying. His tip hit my prostate, and a wave of pre-cum flowed out of me. My cock was getting so sensitive, and the pressure was increasing and felt great, so great that I wanted more, more, more.

"Harder," I said, with my tongue deep inside Jake.

Shawn increased he speed and his depth. At first it hurt, but the burn turned into desire, and he knew it. He doubled his speed and entered me to the hilt. His balls bounced off my ass he pulled back out and plunged back in.

"Yes, yes, yes," I moaned.

Jake increased his rate on my cock, and I knew I didn't have long.

I bore into his butt one more time and felt his balls convulse on my chin. A hot wet spray flowed over my chest and belly. My cock let loose and exploded from the opposite direction. Cum covered my body as Jake still milked my cock and Shawn plowed into my ass. Over and over, he pounded into me, starting another orgasm to flow out of me.

Shawn thrust into me one more time and I felt his cock expand as he shot his hot load. He pulled out and ripped off the condom and shot another load over my body. His thick, black cock spasmed a few more times as he shot out a few more ropes of cum.

Jake flopped on the bed next to me as Shawn lay across my cum-covered body. Sweat and cum dripped from all three of us, as we lay in a gasping heap.

Shawn rolled off of me and lay on his back, his cock still hard. His breathing returned to normal.

Jake rolled out of the bed and headed for the bathroom. He returned with warm, wet washcloths to clean us up.

I wiped away the cum and watched as Shawn cleaned up his massive cock. "Thanks for the best birthday ever."

"Let's head downstairs and have cake." Jake suggested, as he handed out robes to each of us.

"Jake's Cake?" I asked.

"It's your cake now." Shawn smiled.

"Well, it's my birthday, and it's only eleven. I hope you planned to stay the night ..." I kissed him.

"With this kind of welcome, I may never leave."

"Jake, we have an extra room, and he is looking for a place ... And you always said I can't return any of my presents that you gave me."

"I guess we'll have to keep him."

And we did.

LOVE FOR HIRE
By Aiden Lovely

Aiden Lovely resides in New Hampshire. Lovely is a freelance writer that has written many stories, which have appeared in many anthologies. Contact him at chaserbane@gmail.com.

"We can't do this here," Aurelien whispered when the black man pushed him against the wall. His body shuddered when the man's fingers loosened his tie and pulled it from behind his collar. The man that enjoyed this uneasy expression on Aurelien's face was named Fabrice, and Aurelien couldn't resist his touch. He slid his lips down Aurelien's pale cheek, skimming the white skin – teasing him. Fabrice pulled back with a sweet smile on his face. "I'm giving you a chance to run away," he said.

Fabrice was the new vice president of the marketing department and the only black man who had ever been this close to Aurelien. He was tall and muscular, dressed in a beige shirt, red tie and a red blazer.

"Hmph," Fabrice grunted and dampened his lips as he leaned in. He pressed them against Aurelien's. Their lips overlapped. His tongue pushed up against Aurelien's, skimmed the roof of the young man's mouth and splashed saliva like a tsunami. A sweet humming noise strained from Aurelien's throat.

Chains of saliva broke as he pulled away. He wanted to command him to go no further, but the words didn't dare touch the air. His lustful desires were written all over his face. When he felt Fabrice's hand wrap around his waist and slip into his pants from the back, he lost the strength to act rationally.

They couldn't do this now. It was too risky. The two were in his office, and even though Fabrice had locked the door minutes after he entered, Aurelien remained uneasy. A faint dizziness teased his

27

mind. His only option was to submit. Once their lips parted again, soft breaths fell in the air.

Fabrice's touch tickled Aurelien's skin. He scattered tiny kisses on the young man's collarbone. Fabrice pressed his mouth on Aurelien's neck. He sucked and nipped the skin, leaving a trail of bruises. Aurelien released a few moans. His arms uncontrollably draped around Fabrice's shoulders. Fabrice felt Aurelien's throbbing cock through his pants. He pressed his knee against it. Aurelien juddered.

"I don't want this," Aurelien's voice was a whisper.

"You're hard."

Aurelien blushed at the sudden words. His body was begging for more. He couldn't remember the last time a man touched him like that. Fabrice cupped his butt cheek. His fingers slid between the muscles. Aurelien gasped. He pressed his hands on Fabrice's chest.

"If we go any further … I can't," his words fell out as fragments. Fabrice then kissed him again. He was weak in Fabrice's arms. His gumption to push the man away diminished.

As his mind succumbed to the man's attempts, he took a sharp breath. The knock on the door startled him. He quickly fixed his clothes as he heard the voice from behind the door. It was his secretary, Bastien, "Aurelien, the meeting will start in about five minutes."

"We can't do things like this anymore," Aurelien whispered.

"Why not?" Fabrice said.

"Hook ups in the workplace are against policy. I only do things like this with boyfriends."

"Why can't I be your boyfriend?" Fabrice taunted. Aurelien made a disgruntle face at Fabrice and walked ahead of him.

Aurelien stood at about five feet six inches in his dress shoes. He wore a tailored suit with a tie and a matching briefcase. His honey hair was shaggy but cut fashionably. His nose was small with freckles lacing the bridge, and his eyes were wide and green. He was the new president of BBTI advertising. He wasn't promoted because of his good looks; he really did have the potential. Aurelien's job was a little different from most advertising companies because he also worked with clients to pitch sales as if he were an account executive. The company was small but still featured all the departments of a full agency.

Aurelien's clothing held the scent of Fabrice's cologne. He wasn't always this way with men. Aurelien was secluded and reserved, but Fabrice had a way of breaking those boundaries. They barely knew each other, so maybe it was the man's lascivious temperament that was Aurelien's weakness. He kept reminding himself that even if they kissed like lovers, it didn't mean anything. They were just acquaintances – nothing more.

Aurelien's past relationships hindered him from even thinking about falling in love again. He was so over all the drama and all the pain. He decided he'd take a break from all that. He didn't know how long the break would last. It could last a year or eternity; but still, he had no intentions of starting a new.

He sat at the head of the table in the conference room. His co-worker Remi sat to his side. Remi was the vice president of Creative services. He was similar to Aurelien, but only in appearance. He was slim like a weasel and adorned in expensive rags. Bastien, Fabrice and a few others sat on the sides as well. The man on the opposite end of table was the bigwig client from a popular dildo company.

The conference room was more daunting than usual that morning. The tension irrupted instantly. The chair squealed when Aurelien ruffled through his papers again. He turned to the client, "I'm sorry, but at this moment, the only documentation I can recover of your preexisting account is inaccurate. Unfortunately, we do not have a pitch as planned."

Aurelien met the stone eyes of the client; he shriveled into his shirt, "My assistant, Bastien was supposed to have a copy ready. It appears we don't have the original or any files of the document on the computer. It's so strange – unbelievable. While that's no excuse …" Aurelien's words were drowned out as the client spoke:

"It's funny how things like this never happened until you became president of this company."

"… I'm sorry," Aurelien quickly said.

"I placed the document on your desk yesterday," Bastien said in his usually innocent squeak of a voice.

"Well is there anyone in this dang facility that was prepared for this meeting? This is it. If I don't hear a pitch in the next few minutes, I'm moving my account. I swear to god. This is a circus you're running, not a business. My commercial needs to air less than two months from now," the client said and then his foot collided with the chair.

"I apologize, please let us reschedule."

"That won't be necessary," Remi said. He slid out the document from the folder in front of him, "I brought a copy with me just in case something like this would happen." When Remi's words stung the air in front of the client, he should've plunged a knife in Aurelien's back to finish the job.

"You're incompetent and this company should not have to suffer from your mistakes," Remi said as he stood up from his seat and slammed his hands on the table.

The sudden noise made Aurelien flinch. His voice was weak when he said, "I am still your superior, and you must treat me with respect."

It was difficult for Aurelien to demand respect when Remi was right. His mistakes were a representation of the company. His unprofessionalism could cost the company its future.

The conference room fell silent. The long table was the only thing between the two now. The other employees were upright in their chairs, waiting to see what would jump off. Aurelien stood with his body as cold as steel and his breath barely escaping his lips.

"This is … so unreal," the words spilled from him.

"We can't afford to lose important clients at your expense. This meeting is over. I'd be more than happy to discuss the current status and pitch with the client in my office," Remi said.

Aurelien looked at all the cold stares and frigid pouts aimed at him. His face became red. Remi headed toward the door with the client following him.

Aurelien slumped over on the table with his elbows pressed against the wood. He heard Bastien's joyous words although he couldn't make out what he was saying. He heard Fabrice say some things, but they came out as mumbles to his ears. He couldn't believe what happened. Of all people, why would Remi have a copy of the pitch, and why did the original and electronic documents vanish? This was so unusual.

"I need a word alone with Aurelien please," Fabrice said, rejecting Bastien's aggressive touch. Bastien ran his small hands down Fabrice's shirt. He then tugged on the tie.

"I'll be at my desk," Bastien said and licked his lips. He slowly stepped backward, staring into Fabrice's eyes. His eyes followed the black man until he disappeared into the lobby.

Aurelien sprung up when he felt Fabrice's large hand rest on his back. He looked at Fabrice.

"Sometimes I feel like I'm being sabotaged," he said, "Why would Remi have a copy of that? I do the sales pitches, and I approve all the drafts, so why would he have a copy of the approved draft while no other copies exist? I just don't understand."

"It was just a mishap. Next time you'll be more prepared."

"There won't be a next time. This is the second time I upset a client. Soon they'll get rid of me."

He turned to Fabrice with tears running down his cheeks, "They'll get rid of me," he repeated as his voice faded to a whisper. Fabrice looked at him with every muscle stiff in his face. He kissed him. Aurelien pulled away.

"We can't do this here. It's against the policy. You'd lose your job if we were to get caught," he said.

"But when you look at me with wet eyes, what am I supposed to do?" Fabrice said. Fabrice then grabbed his wrist and pulled him close. When Fabrice fastened his lips again, Aurelien didn't have the strength to resist. A nagging groan strained his vocal chords as their tongues were entangled in a wild game of cat and mouse. The scent of his cologne – warmness of his body – Aurelien was losing himself. His body was succumbing to the man's touch. Drowsiness weighed down his eyelids. He wrapped his arms around Fabrice's back and wrinkled the fabric with his gripping fingers.

Fabrice slipped his hands down Aurlien's trousers.

"W-what do you think you're doing?" Aurelien's voice was a faint coo.

"Making you feel good," Fabrice said and then squeezed Aurelien's balls.

"I'm not ready for this," Aurelien said. He managed to push Fabrice away. Fabrice took a step back, watching the disheveled Aurelien fix his clothes. Aurelien hesitated at first. He gave a look of something only he understood with his mouth opened as if words were going to pour out, but nothing did. He grabbed his papers and walked toward the door, "I didn't hire you to be my lover, so don't try to be," he said before the door closed behind him.

Aurelien watched Fabrice work from where he sat in his office. He shook his head and focused on his computer screen. A client – the important Mr. Montague from the popular coffee company was scheduled for next week. He couldn't afford to look unprofessional again. He kept reflecting on the meeting that morning. He was embarrassed to show his face in front of his colleagues. He then looked at Fabrice again; now the man was talking with Bastien.

Aurelien avoided eye contact with Fabrice as he shut the door to his office. What was it about the man that lulled him into submission so easily? Why were they engaging in this kind of relationship?

He leaned against the door. His heart had been hurt so many times. He wasn't ready to try again. It wasn't the difference in color between them that altered Aurelien's actions. He was scared.

"Was Fabrice always this affectionate or did he have an ulterior motive?" Aurelien thought as he sat at his desk. He heard rumors that

Fabrice used to date his ex-boss at his previous job. Many rumors had already spread since his arrival. He couldn't keep his mind off the man since that morning's encounter. His lips still tingled from where Fabrice kissed him. He couldn't concentrate on work. Maybe this was the reason Remi got the best of him. He couldn't let himself be so vulnerable. He already overheard talk among the employees about Remi wanting his position. He inhaled sharply. The frustration brewed in his mind.

He approached the water dispenser in the lobby. From where he stood, he saw Bastien rubbing Fabrice's arm while talking about jargon. What did Fabrice really want? A raise? A fuck buddy? His heart wasn't a play toy. Some people would do anything to get ahead. Aurelien couldn't blame Fabrice for his mistakes. He just couldn't let things like this distract him from his work anymore.

When Aurelien felt a new coldness run on his hand, he realized his cup was overflowing. He couldn't recall when Bastien had approached him either.

"Aurelien, are you okay?"

"I'm fine. It's just water," Aurelien said.

"I know, but you we're daydreaming for a while. A lot seems to be on your mind. Sometimes when I feel cluttered, I take a walk. Y'know, relax with fresh air."

"Yeah. That's a good idea," Aurelien said, "I'm going on lunch."

He took one last look at Fabrice from across the corridor. When his eyes met with Fabrice's deep brown eyes, he was thrown into a frenzy of feelings. He imagined the man's touch on his body. He hurried out of the building, trying to erase those lewd thoughts.

He couldn't take his mind off Fabrice even when he was out of the office. He sat in the small diner across the street with his appetite only big enough to take in a cup of coffee. He returned a few minutes early. He noticed Fabrice and Remi standing in front of his office. He couldn't hear what they were saying. Maybe it was just friendly chit-chat, but they looked as if they were engulfed in a deep conversation.

Remi stood there, dressed in some name brand clothes, and Fabrice was leaning into him. The sight caused unconscious anger to well up inside Aurelien. He stormed over there.

"Fabrice. In my office. Right now," Aurelien said.

"Hmph," Remi said to Fabrice, "And don't question me like that ever again."

He walked past them. Remi's attitude only made Aurelien even angrier with Fabrice. What would Fabrice have asked him that would make him respond like that? Knowing Remi, every word uttered was said in a rude tone though.

"Why were you talking to him?" Aurelian said with the door of his office closed.

"It was business related."

"Yeah, whatever."

He sat at his desk with a pout like a child.

"Remi was coming out of your office when I spoke to him."

"So that's your excuse for flirting with him? He doesn't have a key to my office."

Before Fabrice could explain, Aurelien's voice became a wail, "What is it that you really want from me? I heard the rumors. I know your game. I've been hurt before, so don't think I don't know guys like you."

Fabrice looked at him in surprise.

"I know what you want. You want a promotion, right? A raise in your salary, more vacation time, a bonus. You think if you screw the boss, you'll get a bonus. I'm on to you, but flirting with Remi – that's just disgusting. You'll screw any guy that lets you," Aurelien said.

He crossed his arms. The two were silent. Fabrice's soft footsteps sent waves through the hard bristles of the carpet. He walked over to Aurelien and stopped when he was only a few inches away. He leaned down, quickly arching his back. His shadow was a blanket covering Aurelien. He extended his fingers to Aurelien's chin. Aurelien looked at him. His hand then collided with Aurelien's face. The jolting pain stung Aurelien's cheek. He was paralyzed for a moment.

"Why can't you understand my feelings for you?" Fabrice said.

Aurelien said nothing. He gasped in shock. Fabrice then kissed him. Aurelien pulled away.

"Don't touch me," he shoved Fabrice, "I don't understand you. You're just playing games with me. If it's a bonus you want, I'll give it to you – just stop all this – please." His request was more of a begging than a command. Tears ran down his cheeks, one after another.

"I love you," Fabrice said.

"Why do you keep saying things like that? It's you. It's you that's messing with my head."

They were silent until Aurelien leaned his head on his desk, "I've never been with a black guy before."

"What does color have to do with letting me love you?"

"Well, it's hard. Culturally, I don't think I could ever handle the backlash of an interracial relationship."

"It's not about what others feel; it's about what we feel."

He ran his fingers through Aurelien's hair. He kissed him again. The young man gave no reaction. He remained limp in his chair. Why wasn't Fabrice disgusted with him for thinking that way? He wanted to ask. Maybe his segregated opinions stemmed from his upbringing in a small town.

Fabrice said nothing as he walked toward the door to exit. As soon as his fingers coiled around the knob, Bastien burst through from the other side. His face was pale as he said, "Mr. Montague from Kitty Coffee is here. He is ready for our pitch."

"What?" Aurelien hopped to his feet, "But that's impossible. The meeting isn't scheduled for another week."

Aurelien attempted to gather the rough drafts of the advertisement sketches to pitch. He didn't find anything that was tailored enough to fit the company's needs. The drafts for the project weren't even approved yet. He couldn't pull anything together. How did this happen? How could something so important slip his mind? He couldn't afford to take another tongue lashing. Maybe he really wasn't the best candidate for this position.

"Aurelien, you can't keep our client waiting. He's growing impatient," Bastien said.

"Ok, send him in."

When the door opened, a tall man dressed in black with a briefcase and few other men entered. Aurelien stood up and greeted them each with a handshake.

"Today, we will not have this meeting in the conference room because as of this moment, the company is undergoing a few difficulties."

"What are you implying?" Mr. Montague questioned. His shadow towered over Aurelien.

"W-what I am implying is that at this moment your project is incomplete, and I would like to reschedule another visit with you."

"What?" the client said, "This is ridiculous. You called me this morning, saying it's urgent that we changed the date of the meeting to today, and now you can't deliver. Time is money, and you're wasting my money."

"What?" Aurelien couldn't believe his ears, "I didn't call you this morning."

"Your name is Aurelien, right?"

"Yes, it is, but I didn't call you. I wasn't informed of your arrival until a few minutes ago."

"This is ridiculous," The client shook his head, "Do you have any idea how far we traveled over your mistake? This is just – I'm done

Marcus Anthony

with this company. I'm moving my account to a place where the president of the company acts like a goddamn president."

"N-no please." Aurelien got on his hands and knees, "No, please, you don't understand – it was a mishap, please."

Mr. Montague stormed out into the lobby with Aurelien trailing behind. He then turned to Aurelien, pointed his finger in his face and said, "You have until tomorrow morning to prove to me why my account should stay with this company."

"Thank you so much, sir. I promise you won't regret it," Aurelien said as the client grumbled curse words and mockeries at the facility. When they left, Aurelien realized how pathetic he must have looked in front of his employees. The workers and other clients had seen his begging. His face was flushed. He slinked back into his office. Even he knew there was no way he'd have a pitch by tomorrow.

He pressed his face into his palm. How could he have made such a big mistake? What did the client mean by he had called earlier? Aurelien would at least remember doing that unless he was losing his mind. Something about this situation just wasn't right. When he looked at his calendar, the client's name wasn't scheduled anywhere. Maybe he needed a break. Forgetting clients, misplacing paperwork – this wasn't the first time either. For almost six weeks after he hired Fabrice, he'd become so disheveled. Was it really Fabrice's advancing on him that was screwing up his head? Then he heard a knock on his door.

"Come in,' he said.

Fabrice entered.

"What do you want?" Aurelien said. He didn't have the strength to oppose the man this time. He shuffled a few papers into his briefcase.

"Just now,"

"Yes, just now everyone saw what a lousy employee I am and probably think I should resign."

"No, just now, I looked on my calendar and that client wasn't scheduled until next week."

37

"He says I called him this morning, which is something I don't recall doing. You see what you do to me? Make me lose my mind. Your love makes me lose my mind."

Aurelien didn't know if his words were a joke or if he was being honest. Right then, Fabrice's presence calmed him. The same kindness that he rejected was the same kindness that relieved him.

"I think something is going on."

"It doesn't matter. Everyone has to push as hard as they can today. I need a pitch by tomorrow."

Aurelien looked around his office.

"Soon this'll be someone else's office," he said with a little laugh attached. He sighed as his pensive eyes looked at Fabrice.

"Don't say that."

"I'm taking the rest of the day off. I left Remi in charge. I will let the other departments know of the current situation. I'll approve the pitch first thing in the morning."

Fabrice walked him out of the office with his briefcase. Aurelien stopped at Bastien's desk.

"Bastien, can you mail this letter out for me? It's a letter of apology to the dildo company about the situation this morning."

"Sure, Aurelien. I'm worried about you, so please try to relax. Let me know if you need anything," Bastien said and smiled.

"Thank you." It was the kind words that Aurelien needed right now.

He handed the letter to Bastien.

"Have a good evening," Bastien said as Aurelian and Fabrice exited. He then slid the envelope through the paper shredder.

The cold air felt nice against Aurelien's skin. It was refreshing since he was in his office most of the time. Fabrice walked him to his car. Fabrice didn't say much. He patted Aurelien on the shoulder.

Fabrice looked as if there were words pent up behind his lips. He leaned in close as if he was going to kiss Aurelien. Aurelien jerked back from him. Fabrice then gripped his arm and pulled him close. The two men stood staring into each other eyes. He assumed Fabrice was going to kiss him. The moment seemed like minutes. Aurelien wanted to say something like "kiss me" or "caress me." He was vulnerable. He wanted Fabrice to make a move on him.

Fabrice's fingers weakened around Aurelian's arm. The warmth diminished as his hand fell back to his side.

"I care about you," was all Fabrice said before he headed toward the building. Aurelien watched him until he disappeared through the door.

Aurelien was lonely. The steam from the water filling the tub greeted his skin as he slid into it. The water engulfed his pale, thin body. There were many things on his mind, but Fabrice was the only thing overpowering everything else. He sighed. What was he really feeling?

"Let me love you," Fabrice had once said. The words played again in his mind. The question was how long would Fabrice wait for him to return his feelings? It was true that Aurelien never fell in love with a black man before, but he never thought poorly of interracial dating either. So what was the problem? Sometimes not even he could understand himself. At times, he wanted Fabrice to leave him alone, and now he'd do anything to feel those warm arms embrace him. He didn't know what he wanted. He shook his head. Fabrice needed a different lover. He could never fulfill Fabrice's desires. He didn't know the extent of Fabrice's love – what was the limit? Was there a limit? So many questions pooled around in his mind. If it were a promotion Fabrice was looking for, he could get one easily without having to seduce Aurelien, so what was his real motive? Aurelien didn't hire him to fall in love with him, but in so many ways, the man was holding Aurelien's heart hostage.

"I love you," the words unconsciously spilled from Aurelien's mouth. Fabrice always said those three words to him so easily. Was that proof that he felt so confident about his feelings that simple things were so easy to say? Aurelien always struggled with saying it. It was difficult. How many times could he give his heart away only to have it thrown back in his face? Fabrice was only making everything more complicated.

Aurelien was scared. He feared a lot of things, but right now, he was afraid that just maybe he had fallen for Fabrice. It was difficult to tell because he was searching for sympathy. He didn't want to confuse his vulnerability with love. He knew Fabrice was different. He was the kind of man that meant his words. Just the feeling welling up inside Aurelien made his heart stir when he thought about the other man – a feeling he couldn't describe just yet. It was cruel to lead Fabrice on. He had no intentions of doing that. Simultaneously, the thought of Fabrice no longer wanting him made his chest tighten.

The water sucked down the drain in a whirlwind motion. Aurelien stepped out. His wet footprints dampened the rug. He wrapped a towel around his waist. There was no time for his thinking about lovey-dovey things. He needed to e-mail Bastien about the current status. His job was on the line here. He cursed himself for getting swept away by thoughts of Fabrice, but he yearned to be in the man's arms.

He sat on his bed and powered on his laptop. He heard faint dog barks from the outside. Every little thing seemed so annoying. He ignored the barking dog, but then more dogs joined at louder volumes until it sounded like an orchestra of barking. What was going on? It was as if every dog in the neighborhood was barking. He stepped outside just to check out what was going on. When he stepped out of his front door, he noticed a tall man dressed in a red blazer walking down the sidewalk, looking around – it was Fabrice. He looked lost. The dog barking continued as Aurelien called out to him.

"Fabrice?" he said.

Fabrice looked up at him and then smiled. He hurried over.

"What are you doing here?"

"Ah … well, I kind of started a ruckus."

"Yeah, I noticed," Aurelien said with a little laugh.

"I couldn't find your apartment exactly and got kinda lost. You're neighbor has a lot of dogs. I don't think they like me very much."

Aurelien chuckled, "Nah, they are really sweet. It's just that the dogs aren't familiar with you."

Fabrice then made a serious face, "Aurelien, tomorrow at the conference, bring this folder with you."

"Huh? Why? I haven't e-mailed Bastien yet to see how the progress is coming."

Fabrice leaned into Aurelien. He felt Fabrice's hot breath brush against his skin. The scent of cologne surrounded him. Their eyes were locked on one another. Aurelien's lips trembled. Right now all he wanted was for the man to steal his breath away.

"Trust me. You have to trust me on this. Please," Fabrice said.

They hesitated for a moment. Any minute Fabrice would embrace his body, he thought.

"I can't stay long, but take this," Fabrice pushed the folder in Aurelien's hands. Fabrice then left Aurelien standing in the doorway of the apartment.

Trust him? Aurelien didn't know if he could. He was barely sure if he could trust Fabrice with his heart. What was going on? Fabrice was still wearing his work clothes, too, so that meant he must have come straight to Aurelien's home right after work. It wasn't a booty call he wanted. That little detail made Aurelien happier than he imagined. He wanted to trust Fabrice, but he was uneasy. Maybe Fabrice really did care about him.

It was clear Fabrice wanted more than just a fuck buddy, Aurelien thought. Loneliness fell over him again. He thought the man was going to kiss him. He wished Fabrice would've captured his lips. Having a boyfriend didn't seem like such a bad idea when he felt like this. The image of Fabrice leaning in, feeling his hot breath brush against him stayed in Aurelien's mind all night until he fell asleep.

41

The morning was filled with tension. The office was in chaos. Aurelien felt the anxiety as soon as he entered the building. He only had time to guzzle his coffee and take his paperwork from Bastien. In his briefcase was also the folder Fabrice gave him. He was too exhausted last night; he never got the chance to look at it.

He rushed into the conference room. Remi rolled his eyes at him. Bastien giggled and pulled out a seat for Fabrice. Aurelien suddenly felt this suspicion that he never noticed before. Something was up with his colleagues.

Mr. Montague sat at the head of the table. Aurelien sat at the opposite end.

"Let's begin," Aurelien said, "Once again, I must apologize for the situation yesterday. I can assure you that it will not happen again, and you can feel confident with this agency."

Aurelien then shuffled through his paperwork. He was nervous – trembling. He didn't have a chance to look over any drafts. He took a breath. The same thing couldn't possibly happen again. He shuddered as he flipped through each paper in the folder Bastien gave him. A bead of sweat ran down his forehead. The room seemed hotter than usually. Losing this client was a big deal. He couldn't afford it. His eyes met Fabrice's. He took another breath. His eyes then greeted the grinning Remi. The smile on his face was potent with venom. Aurelien gulped.

"What's taking so long with the pitch? Aren't you prepared?" Mr. Montague said with his arms crossed.

Aurelien said nothing. He shuffled through the papers again. He held his breath. Where was the rough draft of the sales pitch? Not again, he thought. This was too much of a coincidence. This was a set up. Unreal.

He shuffled through the paperwork again. It wasn't there. No matter how many times he flipped through the folder that one paper was missing. In fact, all the papers in the folder had nothing to do with Mr. Montague. It was a hodgepodge of old rough drafts and sketches from previous projects. What was going on?

"You don't have it? This is ridiculous," Remi instigated.

"Um ... well," Aurelien didn't know what to say. The only other folder he had was the one that Fabrice gave him. He knew one thing for sure, Bastien or someone had set him up, and he could tell it wasn't the first time. He couldn't trust any of them. He was the player, and they were the game. He glanced over at Fabrice. Fabrice nodded to him. Somehow the gesture relieved him. "Trust me," Fabrice's words played in his mind. Was there something Fabrice knew that he didn't? Did he know about this set up?

Aurelien took a breath.

"Sorry for the inconvenience," he said with a trembling voice. He had no other option but to trust Fabrice at that moment. He retrieved the folder out of his briefcase. He wanted to trust Fabrice. So much was on the line now. He eased open the folder, holding it by the corner, his heart beating so quickly he felt it in his throat. The excitement jolted through his body.

His words weaseled out from between his lips in a shuddering pitch as he said, "Here's the sales pitch for your new coffee commercial. Imagine a man in the morning, groggy. One can tell just from the expression on his face that he's had a rough night or maybe a fight with his boyfriend. He's almost so exhausted that he can't see straight, but he wanders through the kitchen, leaves his house in his pajamas and walks like a zombie through the streets. He finally enters a supermarket selling Kitty's Coffee. He doesn't bother to pay or find a cup; instead, he rips open a bag and shoves the grounded coffee into his mouth. Then he instantly wakes up and realizes what he's doing. He looks around nervously and then the narrator says 'Kitty Coffee, the instant wakeup call.'"

When he looked up from the paper, the room was silent. Then Mr. Montague spoke in a calm tone, "... I like it. I like it a lot. It captures the concept I was aiming for. Very good."

"At this time we can add any modifications ..."

Before Aurelien could finish his sentence, Remi interrupted him, "How the hell did you get that paper? Tell me now." Remi slammed his fist against the table, and his face twisted in surprise and anger.

"Did you think you could make me look like a fool again?" Aurelien taunted, "I'm not sure what's going on, but I do know there is something suspicious about you, Remi."

"The game is over. You've been sabotaging Aurelien and I wasn't going to let it happen again," Fabrice interjected.

"F-Fabrice ..." the name spilled from between Aurelien's lips. This was why Fabrice came to his home last night. It was to protect him. He must have done a lot of work to get that final rough draft. Aurelien's heart fluttered. Fabrice had done all this to save him.

"Remi, I'm going to have to fire you if I do find that you have been sabotaging the company," Aurelien said.

"That's bullshit. You don't deserve your position; I do. I'm done working under you."

"That's no excuse to sabotage me. It was you who called Mr. Montague, and it was you who rigged that last meeting. I don't know how you were capable of doing these things, but I know you were behind it."

Then he realized it. Bastien, but why? Bastien handled all the paperwork that was given to Aurelien. Bastien had access to his office as well. That was it. It would only make sense that Remi was only capable with Bastien's help.

Aurelien shot Bastien a dirty look. Bastien cowered in his seat. Aurelien wanted to ask him why he would be part of this sabotage. He couldn't wrap his mind around it.

"How can you possibly fire me when you're already violating the policy?" Remi said with a sick smile pulling from the corners of his mouth, "I know exactly what's been going on. You and Fabrice are having an affair. That's right. I knew the entire time. I'm going to report it," he licked his lips, "Say goodbye to this job of yours because it'll soon be mine."

He looked at Remi, "... It's true. I have been having an affair with Fabrice, but I'll tell you something. You can have my job. You can cheat your way to the top, but when I have Fabrice by my side, you can never take away my happiness."

The sudden words surprised everyone.

"Are you happy now, Remi, you got your way? I'll notify the chairman myself," Aurelien said. He then walked out of the conference room.

Aurelien confessed about his affair on the answering machine of the chairman's office some hours ago. He wasn't sure if he should begin cleaning out his office or not. He doubted Remi could handle his position.

His office had grown special to him. So many memories. He threw it all away. He didn't regret it. It was bittersweet.

It was funny how he couldn't recall when exactly he had fallen for Fabrice. Love was like that. It wasn't about color or gender; it was just some unexplainable feeling that just happened on its own. He sighed and took a seat at his desk. This could be the last day he'd ever see these four walls. It wasn't as if he didn't do anything too bad; he'd find another job, maybe something with a less hostile environment. He wouldn't have to deal with Remi, but he'd miss seeing Fabrice. His opinion was different now. He thought an interracial relationship wouldn't work out, but now he longed to be with Fabrice more than he ever dreamed.

Before he could call the chairman again, he heard a knock on his office door. He eased it open. It was Fabrice. After everything he said, how could he face Fabrice without shying away?

"Hi," he said.

Fabrice closed the door behind him.

"I'm surprised you're still here. It's late," he said as he pulled down the shades. It was already the time of day where the streetlamps watched over the streets.

"We are the only employees on this floor," Fabrice said.

"What are you implying?"

Fabrice undid his tie.

"Well, this is probably my last night in this office."

"You didn't hear the good news, did you?"

"What good news?"

Fabrice chuckled, "Remi was fired today. After you left, Mr. Montague said he was moving his account from the company if you were fired. He doesn't trust Remi with his account. They got into an argument, and Mr. Montague recognized Remi's voice from the message he left the other day when he pretended to be you. You probably didn't hear from the chairman because Bastien didn't send the call through to you. Even Mr. Montague found Remi's actions just as disgusting as I did."

Aurelien smiled. A tear escaped his eye as he pressed his face against Fabrice's chest. He couldn't find the words to convey the feeling swirling inside his body. Fabrice wrapped his arms around him. "Give it to me," Aurelien said in a whisper.

Beads of sweat ran down his forehand. He didn't bother to wipe them away. His bare body lay on top of his desk, exposing his throbbing cock and all the marks Fabrice left on his skin. The paperwork was scattered across the floor along with his clothes.

Fabrice pinched and toyed with Aurelien's nipples. His breath shifted in all directions. His body trembled when the cold air surrounded him. As he managed to push more words than a gasp out of his mouth; his lips were then ceased by Fabrice's. His voice leaked out as a humming.

Aurelien was positioned with his legs apart. Both bodies were sweaty. When their lips parted, Fabrice brushed Aurelien's hair back from his forehead.

"Your body is so beautiful," he said.

"Don't say things like that. It's embarrassing," Aurelien struggled to say through his moans. He felt Fabrice's heated hands sliding up and down the shaft of his cock. He wanted Fabrice to devour him more and more. His body yearned for the touch of another man. He

46

was so desperate, he couldn't control himself with Fabrice so close to him.

"Are you ready for me?" Fabrice said. Aurelien bucked his hip. He didn't need to respond in words. Instead he limply wrapped his arms around Fabrice's shoulders and pulled him close to where their bodies were almost symmetrical. He pressed his lips against Fabrice's. The kiss was soft – almost just a touch. He then parted his lips.

Seeing the disheveled Aurelien, hot and bothered, was all the invitation Fabrice needed. He coated his cock in lube and ran his wet fingers inside Aurelien's hole. Aurelien groaned. His body felt on fire.

Fabrice's deep colored cock penetrated the contracting hole in one powerful thrust. A wail tore from between Aurelien's lips. His fingers clinched into fists. The burning sensation of his anus was filled with pleasure. His hole stretched to take in the intruding meat. He ran his fingers through Fabrice's textured hair.

Fabrice grunted and pushed in deeper. He thrust back and forth, releasing ragged breaths. His strong thighs flexed with his every move. At that moment, Aurelien felt as if his body was melting.

His voice poured out in chunks. It was getting harder and harder to control himself. He clinched his teeth together. He struggled to say "I'm going to come."

He lifted his torso up with the support of his hands. His hand then slipped on the polished oak wood, causing him to lose balance and allowing Fabrice's cock to slip in deeper. His head hit the desk, and another moan escaped his mouth.

Fabrice caressed his body. The touch of the warm fingertips felt so good on his fevered skin. He closed his eyes. Their bodies bounced in harmony. He massaged his own swollen cock, begging for a release. Fabrice was a beast on him. He was jerked back and forth. Fabrice's tongue lashed out at him before he could moan again. Soon his moaning lips were captured by the sexy black man. His legs wrapped around Fabrice's lower body. Fabrice was consuming him.

Sweat glistening like diamonds laced his pale cheeks as he lay with delicate skin and fragile eyes. His eyelashes were thick brushes of black; they fluttered like butterfly wings as his face soaked up the pain. He drifted in a sea of pleasure, almost feeling oceanic when the pleasure overwhelmed him. No words squeezed from his lips, just moans. His fingers scraped at the wood as they did a passionate dance on his desk. Aurelien had never looked so beautiful before that moment.

The friction of their bodies and the sloppy noises of Fabrice's ball slamming against him filled his ears. Their lips met once again. Fabrice was so warm and heavy. As his speed increased, Aurelien was ready to burst. Fabrice pummeled him. Aurelien could no longer hold back. His limbs became limp. He jerked, grunted and climaxed. His cum splattered on Fabrice's abdomen. Then, he moaned when he felt Fabrice's warm jizz splash inside him and heard a groan from above.

The sperm rolled out of his bottom as he lay there with his chest heaving up and down. Fabrice slumped on top of him, his cock growing soft and cum running off the head. He brushed Aurelien's hair out of his face again and said, "I love you."

"It's hard to say but I feel different inside."

"But this wasn't your first time with a man."

"Not like that. Like I said, it's hard to describe, but I feel different like everything I thought I knew was wrong. Thank you."

"Don't thank me. I protect those I love."

Aurelien looked at him with wide eyes. This man ... he was completely different in color, but his loving heart was the same as Aurelien's. It was true; everything he knew had been erased. All that nonsense about interracial love was jargon – love was love – race, gender, nothing mattered, but the feelings they shared. Aurelien felt his heart pound so loudly in his chest. He imagined that Fabrice's heart was beating just as loudly.

"You know, I never imagined falling in love again after all the other guys ..."

"I'm not like the other guys," Fabrice said and put his big hand on Aurelien's chest.

"I love you ..." the words slipped from Aurelien's mouth. Fabrice smiled at him. Neither of them exchanged another word. They just stared at each other until Fabrice pressed his lips against Aurelien's. Aurelien wrapped his arms around Fabrice's shoulders. He wished he could bask in this warmth forever. He had learned so much since he hired Fabrice. It was as if he hired a lover instead of a colleague.

RACE
By Jay Starre

Residing on English Bay in Vancouver, Canada, Jay Starre has pumped out steamy gay fiction for dozens of anthologies and has written two gay erotic novels. Contact Jay Starre on Facebook.

Troy braced himself with his bare feet planted firmly against the mat of real grass that grew on the floor of the 981Z Sundazzle. The car was a prototype, and his pal Race had invited him out on this wild test drive with him.

The hood was down, and the salt-laden air off the Pacific washed over him in a cool rush of tingling sensation up and down his body. Especially, since he was totally naked.

"Tell me again why we had to be butt-naked for this crazy fucked-up test drive?"

Although the car itself ran with an eerie quiet, the rush of air blowing past them at sixty-five miles per hour was anything but. His shouted question whipped away behind them.

"You'll see soon enough! What a ride, huh? Hold on to your seat!"

There was no reason to worry about holding on. The seat belt had strapped firmly in a tight X across his chest while a pair of similar dark brown leather straps had secured his thighs just above his knees. He was effectively bound in place, legs spread and back pressed against the ultra-smooth rubberized seat.

They had climbed into the glittering emerald-green vehicle only a few minutes earlier at Race's shop just outside of Monterey. No one had been around to see them both strip and board, with Race guffawing, and Troy rolling his eyes. His friend was not only an eccentric genius, he was kinky, too, and always seemed to get Troy into

51

these outrageous situations. College buddies, they were still best friends five years later even though Race was a crazy inventor and Troy a staid investment banker.

He counted on Race to add some thrills to his life. He'd gone along with the naked shit because he really wanted to ride in the cool car, and because Race was one hot stud, regardless of his nerdy personality.

Now, he was second-guessing that decision.

He wasn't regretting the naked part; it felt kind of cool being in the buff and strapped into a spaceship-like car out under the glorious summer sunshine of the California coast. But Race was driving like a maniac!

Barely a mile from the inventor's studio-lab, they had breezed past the entrance to Ford-Toyota's private test road that meandered along the cliffs above the Pacific Ocean for nearly forty miles. It was an old highway closed down in 2020 once the newer freeway had been built above.

Grass had replaced pavement, which supposedly was the future of all highways once these new floater-vehicles came into mass production. The Sundazzle had no wheels; it ran on a cushion of air.

The car hugged the roadway at two feet above the ground. The roadway had to be level and without obstruction, but need not be constructed of pavement. Grass was the intended new paving material for highways across America. The green folks were chomping at the bit to get this new technology up and running.

"Fucking awesome, huh?" Race shouted as he yanked on the steering wheel, and they careened around a tight corner.

Troy didn't know what to say. He was frightened out of his wits! He looked over at his friend, noting the huge grin and the wide excited eyes. Race had a really big goofy smile and huge dark eyes. He also had one big fucking black cock, which Troy couldn't help noticing was sticking straight up from his lap.

Troy's view of that hard-on was partially obscured as his long blond hair whipped chaotically around his cherubic pink face. His own looks were pretty well the opposite of Race's, with his ivory-pale skin and blue eyes and petite features, but his cock was on a massive scale to match his pal's, although it was fat instead of long. Regardless of his fear, once he got a look at his crazy friend's monster boner, his own began to fatten up between his spread thighs.

He wondered, though, if Race's boner was only because he was getting off on the car and the speed and the danger, or if there was something more.

There was something more.

"If you think this is amazing, get a load of what else this baby can do for you!"

They careened around a hair-pin turn as Race shouted out that enigmatic statement. A moment later, the blond banker began to realize what that something more entailed.

"What the fuck?" he shouted

Between his legs, in fact between his bare butt-cheeks spread over the rubberized seat, something began to slowly rise out of the seat's surface. Slippery and sinuous, the column of lubricated rubber traced its way upward between his cheeks, sliding back and forth until it found what it sought.

His asshole!

"Don't tell me this car's got fucking automated dildos!"

"You bet! Programmed to find your hole and slide right in! Enjoy the ride! Yee-haw!"

Race slammed the accelerator pedal to the floor and the car leaped ahead straight down the narrow highway toward the Pacific Ocean at ninety miles per hour.

The dildo knew what it was doing! As Troy let out a shriek of animal fear, that snaking rubber toy tapped at his clamping sphincter while squirting a steady stream of lubricant. His thighs were strapped in place, and there was nothing he could do but accept the inevitable.

Not that he minded; it certainly seemed to be taking his mind off the headlong race down the highway toward another hair-pin turn, and either making that turn, or crashing into the Pacific off a cliff!

With the rush of ocean air shrieking past, he gulped in his fears. Exhaling deeply, he relaxed his asshole and allowed that invading rubber cock to slide past his trembling butt-lips.

"How's that feel? I can control how deep and how hard it fucks with this dial!" Race shouted as he reached out to the dash and took hold of a bright red knob there.

"Watch the fucking road! Hell ... yeah ... that is fucking deep!"

The dildo thrust up inside him as Race twisted the knob. There was plenty of lube, some of it coating his bare ass-cheeks and the seat beneath him. That was a total turn-on, his ass sliding around in the lube as that slithering dildo drove up into him. He braced himself with his bare feet against the grassy floor and held on for dear life.

Amidst the fear and the gut-churning sensation of getting fucked up the ass, he couldn't help thinking one thing. There was no way Ford or Toyota was planning on adding this feature to their standard models!

Race echoed his thought. "I fucked around with the specs and added this little option all on my own. Wild, huh? Fucking wild!!"

The idiot laughed hysterically as he manipulated the knob on the dash and slammed on the brakes as they approached the turn ahead and the possibility of imminent death. The dildo pumped in and out of Troy's ass with frantic strokes, slamming his prostate and rubbing his tender ass-lips with maddening friction.

He couldn't help but squirm down over the irresistible pumping pleasure even as he braced himself and said his prayers. The wide Pacific Ocean yawned before them, a hundred feet below.

"Hell yeah!" Race shouted as he spun the wheel expertly and they tore around the corner.

They didn't careen over the edge, even though the tail end of the Sundazzle whipped back and forth in a crazed dance and the front end did its own whiplash until Race got it under control a moment later.

Now they were headed up instead of down, a series of gut-churning twists and turns visible ahead. Troy's heart raced and his pulse pounded, while his asshole continued to receive a thorough ramming – and he was strapped to the seat helpless to escape it.

Tearing his eyes from the dizzying view, he glanced at Race beside him. The stud's enormous cock jerked and leaked a steady stream of gooey pre-cum. The pale nut cream was shiny over the midnight black knob which leaped and twitched continually. Obviously, the dildo up his sexy black ass was providing him some sweet pleasure, too!

"There's more, Bro."

Breathless, he shouted back. "What more? Does this thing suck cocks, too?"

Race just laughed as he spun the wheel again, and the Sundazzle whipped around another corner. He stepped on the accelerator and moved his hand from the dildo knob to one beside it. He pushed it in and a green light began flashing. Troy wriggled around over the pumping dildo and gripped the seat's armrests as he contemplated what nasty trick the Sundazzle was about to perform.

He found out a moment later. From the front of his seat between his spread legs, a cylindrical object rose upwards. Attached to a flexible metal cord, it danced in the air above his lap for an instant before it swerved and darted directly for his cock.

Open at the end, it found the flared crown of his hard-on and swallowed it up. Slowly, it began to slither downwards in a gulping descent.

"What the hell?" He yelped.

"Nice, huh? It's full of warm lube. I'll turn it up," Race shouted.

There was one of the same things fastened to his own lap. The tubes were constructed out of a translucent flexible material, and both their cocks could be seen beneath the murky exterior. His fat pink own throbbed within the juicy interior while Race's black one pulsed inside his own.

The end of that big tube slithered slowly downward, gulping up inch after inch of cock as it headed for his balls. The insides were steamy warm with an inner coating that massaged his cock-head and shank with pulsing waves. And meanwhile, the dildo up his ass pumped in and out without missing a beat.

The car was both fucking him and sucking him!

He looked over at Race and noticed his look of rapt ecstasy. His big grin split his face nearly from ear to ear, his white teeth flashing between his big red lips. His dark face flushed almost purple. His eyes were so huge it looked as if they were about to pop out of his head.

"Can you drive? Can you fucking drive with a dildo up your ass and that thing attached to your cock?" Troy yelled.

He sure as hell couldn't imagine trying to drive. How was Race doing it?

"Hell yeah! I love it! Let's see what this little baby can do!"

Troy groaned. What hadn't it done already? He gripped his armrests, gritted his teeth and settled in for the ride. There wasn't much else he could do.

Race slammed on the brakes before every turn and booted it afterwards. The car performed without a hitch. Its silent motors, powered by solar panels embedded in the emerald-green paint and covering every inch its surface, forced air from jets in the base that either propelled it forward, or slowed it down when their direction was reversed. Highly computerized gyroscopic stabilizers kept it from rocking too violently or turning over.

Fucked up the ass and being massaged by a juicy mechanical snake, Troy leaned back and gasped and grunted, staring ahead at the grassy highway, the looming cliffs, the wide Pacific and endless blue skies. It was truly mind-boggling.

Regardless of the recklessness of his driver buddy, he was forced to respect his capabilities. He seemed to have utter control over the Sundazzle. And not only that, he had a real knack at manipulating the sex features, too!

Laughing and shouting, Race twisted the dials back and forth. The red one increased the speed of the ramming dildo up their asses, or slowed it down to a deep gut-massage that had Troy aching and squirming. The green one had the translucent sleeve encasing his cock pulsing either faster or more slowly, while also either slackening its grip or tightening it.

The sleeve had slithered down to his balls and his entire fat shank was trapped within it. Lube leaked out all over his smooth nut-sack and more lube coated the seat between his wriggling ass-cheeks.

Race obviously experienced the same pleasures. His muscular dark arms reached out to grip the steering wheel and fool around with the sex dials while his big black thighs were strapped to his seat like Troy's, but his bare feet were each planted on a pedal, one for the brakes and one for the accelerator. His powerful black chest was strapped back against the emerald-green seat like Troy's as well.

Drool coated his plump red lips while tears of pleasure leaked from the corners of his eyes. He was getting off, and getting off good. He looked over at Troy and winked while twisting the red dial violently, which sent the dildo planted up his blond buddy's ass to quivering wildly.

"Fuck! What the hell is going on now?" he yelped.

"It vibrates, too! Awesome, huh? Hold on, Bro, for an about-face!"

Hold on? What the fuck did he think Troy was doing? All he could do was groan as the dildo in his ass vibrated and wriggled like a rattlesnake and the sleeve slurped on his fat hard-on. Even though he'd been warned, he still shrieked when Race yanked on the wheel, and the jets beneath them rearranged themselves in perfect synchronization.

They spun around and around. Race shouted as Troy screamed and the dildos up their asses danced. Fortunately, they were at a wide spot in the road and neither plummeted off the edge below or smashed into the hillside above. Three crazy spins and they righted themselves, heading in the opposite direction.

"Fucking awesome!"

Troy's head was still spinning, and his heart was practically in his throat, but he was also totally exhilarated. As Race stepped on the accelerator again and they lurched forward, Troy settled back into his rubberized seat and gave in to the twin sensations bombarding his stuffed ass and encased cock.

After that crazy performance, Troy found himself also surrendering to Race's expertise. He was driving like a maniac, but he seemed to know what he was doing. The blond banker allowed himself to gulp in the salt air that rushed past them while relishing the speed of the car beneath him.

That's when Race really showed his expertise. Not only did he whip them around turns at breakneck speed, but also he manipulated the dials on the dash to give Troy one hell of a fuck and suck job.

Lying back and wallowing in the sensations, he soon found himself floundering toward orgasm. "Hell yeah! Keep that up, and I'm going to blow, Race," he shouted.

"How's this? Enough to get you off, Bro?" Race shouted back as he twisted the knobs on the dash.

The dildo up his ass not only vibrated at a gut-churning pace, it also wormed its way deeper than ever. How long was the fucking thing? And the sleeve around his cock sucked so powerfully he thought he was being pulled inside out.

They headed straight down-hill with the Pacific Ocean ahead, and the sun a golden ball hovering just above the horizon.

He let himself go, surrendering totally. That was enough. "I'm shooting! I'm fucking shooting while this fucking car fucks me good!"

Orgasm rocked him. His cock spewed into the vacuuming sleeve while his asshole quivered around the vibrating dildo buried in his gut. The wind whipped his hair back as the Sundazzle braked viciously, and they spun off the road and into a wide spot.

They stopped. Cum still spurted from his cock as that dildo churned in his ass. He felt awash in lubricant, sweat and jizz. He looked straight out over the blue ocean and into the red ball of the sun just hitting the water in its final descent.

"Did you come, too?" he asked between gasps for breath.

Race was grinning still from ear-to-ear. But there was something in his look that warned Troy there was more to come. "Not yet. But I'm planning on it."

He pushed in the two knobs. Their lights went out, and immediately, the sleeves over their cocks withdrew while the dildos up their asses slithered out and back into the seats beneath them. Race pushed in another knob and the seatbelts strapping them both to their seats snapped open and slid back into their compartments.

"A little romance to end the day won't hurt. How about it?"

The big black inventor crawled over to straddle his blond pal, then with that nasty grin in place, pushed in the knob on the arm of his seat. It immediately reclined to throw Troy backwards with Race on top of him.

The crazy driver grabbed the backs of Troy's knees and shoved them forward. Without missing a beat, he rammed his huge black cock deep into the blond's asshole. At the same time, he bent down and planted his plump red lips over Troy's.

They did what lovers had done probably since the car was invented. Parked by the side of the road, overlooking the ocean and the setting sun, they fucked.

Troy felt as if he'd just run a marathon race and was totally relaxed. His asshole oozed lube from the dildo and his entire butt and crotch was coated with it. So was Race's. They slithered together in the lube and cum and sweat as Race kissed and fucked Troy with relentless passion.

That huge black cock seemed much bigger than the Sundazzle dildo that had just fucked him, but maybe it was just his imagination, or the way Race used it to probe deep, yank out, tease the dripping entrance with the flared head, then slowly slide all the way in again while twirling his tongue around inside Troy's mouth.

He kept that up, teasing Troy's asshole, then pounding it, then slowly pumping it again before revving it up and going for the final, thrusting culmination. The inventor shouted out his release and pumped a full load into his buddy's churning asshole.

The blond couldn't help himself. With the heat of a real cock up his ass, the feel of a real, live warm body covering his, and Race's plump soft lips over his and stabbing tongue delving deep, he blew his second wad of the afternoon.

They cuddled together as the stars came out and chatted about the possibilities of the new vehicle. Apparently, even though Ford was the largest car conglomerate in the world, they needed financing for the experimental venture. That's where Troy came in. He had the connections to ensure massive funding.

"Is that why you brought me on this little adventure? I thought it was because we're best friends, and you like to fuck me. By the way, does this car run in the dark? There's obviously no sunlight to charge the solar cells."

"I forgot to mention that. I guess we're stuck here till morning. That will give you lots of time to make a decision about financing. And time for some more cock in the ass."

Race was still on top of him and staring down into his eyes in the soft light of the stars. After years of friendship, Troy could tell when his pal was lying. The car could run in the dark, or else it wouldn't be very useful. He just wanted to fool around some more.

That was fine with him. He reached down to cup the cheeks of Race's ass. The mounds were smooth and huge. The crack was deep, and in that crack, he found a juicy hole well-lubed by the car's amazing dildo. He slid a trio of fingers into that deep pit and twisted them.

Race squirmed and bleated, "Hell yeah! My turn to get fucked!"

And that's exactly what Troy had in mind. He'd decide about the investment shit later. Now it was time to fuck some big beautiful black ass!

THE NORSEMAN AND THE NUBIAN
By Jay Starre

Harold the Norseman perched silently on a lip of rock that overhung the burbling stream below. It was a fine spring morning in the Year of Our Lord 910. Harold was a Christian, albeit a nominal one. It suited his purposes as a trader in the wider world to adhere to such a popular religion.

The tall man was a warrior as well as a trader and he was well-armed and alert as he gazed at the lone man bathing in the waters below. He had never seen such a man in all his life. Even though this was his third journey to Constantinople, the capital of the mighty Eastern Roman Empire, he had only laid eyes on black men from a distance and in a crowd.

Never had he seen one naked.

His prick reared beneath his fur-trimmed trousers to throb against the soft leather. The man was standing knee deep in the blue-green water as it flowed swiftly past and lathering himself with a bar of some kind of soap.

He was tall, perhaps even taller than Harold himself. His back was broad, and his shoulders swelled with power. A narrow waist accentuated the rounded swell of a pair of stupendous buttocks. His flesh was black as obsidian.

Harold slid a hand down into his trousers to massage his stiff tool as he gazed at those big arse cheeks and imagined them spread wide. As if God himself was of the same mind, the black man bent over to reach into the flowing water and splash himself with cold water.

His wide-spread feet were planted firmly in the uncertain bed of wet pebbles. In that bent position, his mighty ass yawned open.

Harold was treated to the sight of a smooth crack – and a dark pouting hole.

He bit back a groan as he pumped his prick and imagined stepping between those parted thighs and ramming his stiff pole deep into that puckered opening. Would the stranger cry out in protest, or would he moan with pleasure?

The man turned around, and Harold let out a startled gasp. His prick! It seemed to drop nearly halfway to his knees and appeared as thick as a man's arm! Black as midnight and hooded, even in its quiescent state, it was a truly formidable weapon.

Harold's own prick oozed out a big dribble of pre-cum, and he moaned aloud. The black stranger looked up, perhaps alerted by the loud moan from above. Across the dozen yards that separated them, their eyes met.

The stranger's hand rose, palm outward. It was a gesture of peace, or welcome. The dark eyes gazed into Harold's, calm and unafraid. The Norseman, all too aware of his hand in his pants, flushed brightly but managed to raise his free hand in a similar gesture.

He made a bold decision. Nodding to the stranger, he turned to begin the steep descent along the side of the high bank. When he reached him a few moments later, the man was still naked and faced him with a calm demeanor.

Harold spoke a dozen languages but chose to try Greek. This was a common trading language, especially when finding oneself within the sphere of the mighty city of Constantinople.

"I am Harold of Sweden"

The black answered without pause, also in Greek.

"I am Saba the Nubian"

"Are you alone?"

"Yes, and you my friend?"

"My ship is moored to the north with my men in attendance. But yes, at the moment I, too, am alone."

They stood so close Harold could smell the Nubian. It was a distinctive odor he recognized as the oil of sesame. It must have been the soap he used, which had to have included the oil and thus lent him a similar aroma. It was mild and nutty – and very earthy and sensual.

The Norseman was a giant, but so was the Nubian. They were a formidable match and eyed each other speculatively.

Harold's flowing hair was a soft honey-gold, as was his beard which was trimmed short, especially around his full-lipped mouth. A strong nose dominated the wide face. Sky-blue eyes under pale brows gazed brazenly out at the world.

The Nubian was clean-shaven with narrow cheeks. A long aquiline nose pointed downward at a generous mouth with plump lips and sparkling white teeth. His eyes were dark and huge.

There sometimes comes a moment when two men see into each other's hearts without either speaking any words to reveal the secret they share. This was one of those times. It was Harold who dared reach out to lay a firm hand on the Nubian's shoulder.

The moment flesh pressed to flesh, they were lost to their needs. The feel of firm and potent muscle beneath his palm and fingers sent a shudder of excitement through the tall Norseman, a shudder the Nubian could not mistake.

His plump lips pursed then gaped wide in a brilliant smile. He reached out and grasped the waist of Harold's trousers, immediately tearing at the strings that laced the fly. With a matching grin, the Norseman reached out with his free hand and seized the thick appendage dangling between the Nubian's powerful thighs.

The prick was hot and turgid. As his fist surrounded it and began to pump, it quickly began to grow. The Nubian's nimble fingers had already unlaced Harold's trousers and were pushing them downward. Out popped Harold's stiff prick.

The dark hands seized it and began to stroke. Harold groaned and leaned forward so that both their pricks touched as his pink one jerked and the Nubian's dark one rapidly assumed its full length.

"What a monster! I would taste it, my new friend!"

"Yes. I would have your sweet lips part for it. On your knees, Norseman."

The chuckle that followed Saba's words softened their demanding tone. Harold, a proud man, in this instance cared little about words as he felt that mighty tool stiffen and pulse under his pumping fist. He dropped to his knees in the dewy grass and faced the immense thing.

With two hands, he gripped the throbbing shank. It was truly enormous! Leaning in, he flicked out his tongue to dab at the exposed head. It was surprisingly slender compared to the massive girth of the shank. Tapered and without hardly any flare, once the hood was pulled down it seamlessly flowed into the giant shaft. Harold shuddered for the second time as he imagined that tapered head slithering up his tender asshole!

He tickled the slit, licking off a sheen of pre-cum as he pumped the shaft with his fists. His pumping hands urged out more of the pre-cum which he licked up greedily. Above him, the Nubian moaned as he thrust against the teasing tongue. He placed his big hands on Harold's honey-blond locks and began to stroke them.

Harold's trousers were tangled in his leather boots down around his ankles, and he was well aware of his exposed thighs and ass. His tunic was sleeveless and revealed tanned arms, but his lower body was pale as milk and coated in a nearly invisible down of blond. The tunic was belted close around his tight waist, which emphasized the swell of his muscular buttocks.

The Nubian must have enjoyed the sight of those naked nether cheeks because his hands quickly dropped down behind Harold to find and begin caressing them.

The feel of those giant hands on his ass only increased Harold's excitement. He opened wide and engulfed the black cock-head with his pink lips. The heated flesh pulsed and jerked as he began to suck on it.

The hands on his bare white ass gripped and squeezed, a testament to Saba's own excitement as his prick was slowly swallowed and steadily pumped. With those massive hands massaging his naked ass, Harold gobbled up inch after inch of the monster black meat until he could get no more of it in his mouth without choking. And he had barely swallowed half of it!

His pumped it more vigorously with his fists as he began bobbing up and down over it. His gurgling slurps and Saba's pants and grunts created nasty music against a backdrop of the burbling stream and buzzing insects.

Their shared excitement increased as Harold bobbed faster and deeper, and Saba's long black fingers insinuated themselves between the kneeling Norseman's plump white ass-cheeks. When they found his puckered hole and began to lightly stroke it, Harold groaned and shuddered, then managed to swallow up another few inches of the massive black cock in his mouth.

That proved the Nubian's undoing. Emitting an explosive grunt, he thrust his hips against Harold's bearded face and let loose a river of nut cream. Harold swallowed it all, sucking the stream of goo into his throat with satisfied glee. It was a sort of triumph to pull a load out of the big Nubian. He reveled in it as he gulped down all the copious seed that was offered.

After every last drop was sucked out of him, Saba let out a deep sigh and straightened up as he released his grip on the Norseman's round ass. His big prick, still stiff, slid out from between Harold's wet lips.

The Norseman wondered what would happen next, but had only a moment to wait before he found out. With a satisfied grin on his face, Saba stepped back a pace and reached up into the low branches of the birch sapling that stood against the high bank beside the grassy shore. A large bag of brightly-colored wool hung there. Out of it, he pulled a slender glass bottle of exquisite design.

"Sesame oil. It is one of the precious items I offer for trade in Constantinople. It has magical qualities. Shall we investigate together this fine magic?"

The smirk and wink that followed set Harold's imagination on fire. He eyed the still-stiff prick slapping against the Nubian's dark belly and imagined it coated in the exotic oil, but this was not what Saba had in mind, at least not immediately.

Instead the giant black man dropped to his knees, then rolled onto his back and lifted his legs. With one arm hooked around a knee, he reached down with the other and upended the bottle of oil over his parted crack.

The glass bottle obviously had a small opening in the tip and oil spurted out in a light stream to run down the dark crack and coat it in a glistening sheen. The oil dribbled down to pool in the dark center of Saba's puckered asshole.

Harold moaned aloud as he scooted forward, still on his knees, frantically kicking off his boots and trousers at the same time before he planted himself half-naked between those raised thighs. His pink cock reared upward in a wicked curve between them. Saba winked as he reached out to splash some of the sesame oil over it. The overhanging birch trees offered some dappled shade from the brilliant sunlight, and Harold's flaming prick glistened brightly where the light hit it.

He moaned as he pushed downward on the head to aim it at the dark opening between Saba's raised legs. The shaft was slender and rigid, but the crown was mushroom-shaped and very blunt. Staring intently at the oiled hole, he began to rub that flared knob all over the slippery anal lips. Pink flesh met black, a startling contrast and an exciting prospect as Harold imagined that flaming crown slowly disappearing into the dark cavern he was testing.

He used his other hand to finger the sleek hole, teasing the spongy entrance while continuing to rub it with his flared cock head. He was amazed at how it pouted outward to meet his attentions, then actually yawned open as the Nubian squirted more oil over his crack and Harold's fingers and cock.

68

He couldn't hold back any longer. He shoved inward. His cock head disappeared between quivering ass lips. Heat enveloped it. He groaned and shoved deeper. Half his pink rod slid inside. He pushed deeper, then even deeper. All at once, his prick was buried to the balls!

It was amazing. The dark hole seemed bottomless. He pulled all the way out with a groan and began all over again. With a bright glint in his blue eyes and an intense grin on his bearded face, he teased the slippery sphincter with slow pumps. His flaming crown slithered inward, then popped back out. Then again, and again.

It was an awesome feeling to have those dark lips cling to his cock head, then part and welcome it in, then hug it again as it slowly withdrew. He glanced up from the fascinating view to see the Nubian smiling as brightly, his lush red lips gaping open like his dark hole. Harold reached up and slid a pair of fingers between the beautiful lips. Saba immediately began to lick and suck on them.

The blond trader groaned as he felt the wet lips surround his fingers. He leaned forward and gored the dark hole with the full length of his prick. Saba met his lunge with a heave of his powerful hips and swallowed him completely. The quivering hole massaged his shank with heated delight.

The broad ass rose off the grass and began to thrust against him. All that dark expanse was beautiful to look at, and Harold used his free hand to stroke the smooth flesh as he continued to finger the Nubian's wet mouth and slam-fuck his eager hole.

The sesame oil truly seemed magical. It was not only slippery but had an intoxicating scent to it. It was as if they were fucking in a pit of woodsy earth, ripe with sensual root and nut and leaf.

The dark hole swallowed him up and wouldn't let him go until he had pumped himself into a frenzy, flaming prick goring midnight black ass, faster and faster, harder and harder.

"I am coming," he shouted.

A river of spunk flooded the Nubian's battered hole as the giant man heaved his mighty ass upwards to trap the spewing prick in his gut and milk it dry. Breathlessly, with heart pounding, he collapsed atop the smooth flesh of his new friend.

Feeling the Nubian's huge pole throbbing along his belly, he realized there might be more to come. Again, he found out rather quickly what that was.

"Come, turn around and sit on my face. I would taste that plump white Norseman ass."

Saba's deep voice and its nasty message sent another shudder through the winded blond's big body. Yes! The Nubian's tongue up his ass would feel amazing; he was sure of it.

Slithering around over the naked black body beneath him, Harold turned head to toe, ending up with his knees planted on either side of Saba's face. His own face was in the Nubian's dark crotch. The mighty prick lay stiff and plump on his smooth belly.

He had sucked it once, and was eager to do so a second time. He gripped the shaft with his hands and raised it to his lips. Just as he engulfed the tapered head with his warm mouth, big hands pulled his ass cheeks apart and a mouth burrowed between the white mounds to smack and lick and suck.

He jerked from head to toe as tongue came out to stroke his puckered hole. Lips clamped over it and began to suck it inside out. He squirmed down over that mouth and grunted as dark cock slithered past his tonsils and into his throat.

Harold felt that giant shank pulsing inside his throat while a tongue stabbed into his quivering asshole. The hot body beneath him writhed sensually as Saba thrust up into his mouth and pulled downward on his ass. Both his holes were being violated!

Then Saba lifted the ass on his face briefly in order to give him another command. "You must do as I do, Norseman. You must eat some ass!"

The man seemed entirely uninhibited, and Harold found his own inhibitions melting away. He allowed the huge shaft in his mouth to slither out, then hooked both hands around Saba's dark thighs and pulled back on them to expose the hole he had just fucked so thoroughly. It pouted outward, dribbling sesame oil and his own cum.

He groaned as he buried his face between the splayed thighs and clamped his mouth over the oozing hole. As Saba pulled back down on his ass and twirled a tongue deep in his own pink slot, he sucked his own cum out of the Nubian's pulsing dark pit.

A hand slid into his parted white crack, and a pair of well-oiled fingers found his hole. Replacing the tongue that had just teased it, they slithered up his hole and probed with twisting insistence. He squirmed around them as a dark hand clamped over one of his white ass-cheeks and held him in place. There was nothing to do but relax over the invasion, and once he did, another finger entered him. The three digits roamed around in his gut, eliciting the most amazing sensations he had ever experienced.

As the trio of sesame-oil coated fingers probed him, he sucked deeply on the Nubian's dark hole and felt his stiff prick throb against his upper chest. He couldn't help but imagine the giant thing replacing those digging fingers!

As if reading his mind, Saba spoke again. "Time to fuck this sweet pink hole. You must sit on my prick, Norseman."

Oh God! Yes, that was what he had wanted from the moment he laid eyes on the dark monster. Pulling out of the dark crotch with a smack of his lips, he rose up and once more slithered over the smooth body beneath him. The fingers up his ass slid out, leaving him oiled and open as he crawled downward to end up perched over the Nubian's belly.

Crouching on his bare feet, he seized the black pole and lifted it to aim at his parted crack. Saba chuckled as he splashed another stream of oil over his dark prick and Harold's pale ass-cheeks.

His hole had already been primed by those oil-coated fingers but more of the oil wouldn't hurt, which was obviously what Saba believed. His dark fingers found the gaping pink hole again and rubbed more sesame oil over the distended lips as Harold aimed the head of his prick at it.

The slender tip easily slipped past the stretched sphincter into the cavern beyond. Both men groaned simultaneously at the heated sensation as quivering ass lips encased pulsing cock head. Encouraged by the ease of that entry, the blond trader began to squat down over the black prick.

"Oh! God above! It is so big," he grunted as the tapered head slid deeper, and the thick shank began to stretch his tender ass-lips.

"Allah be praised, your hole is so hot and juicy!"

The stuffed sensation was so exciting, along with Saba's breathlessly nasty words, Harold determined to take more. He hadn't been able to swallow it all with his mouth, but he would attempt to gulp it all up with his asshole!

Sesame oil dribbled around the straining pink ass lips and glistened around the black shaft as it slowly disappeared, inch after inch. Saba's big hands gripped the Norseman's broad hips and pulled downward on them as his own dark hips rose up off the grass.

Harold was slowly impaled! The shank only grew fatter as it neared the base. He shook from head to toe as his pale ass dropped closer and closer to the Nubian's dark belly. There was no rushing it, but there was no pause either as that giant pole steadily slithered deep into Harold's quivering gut.

"Oh! Oh! I have it all!"

"Yes! You have taken every inch!"

Together, they succeeded in burying the mighty prick entirely up Harold's oiled slot. His round ass flushed bright pink against the dark belly he sat on. His own prick curved upward in a throbbing arc between his splayed thighs. He was stuffed full, and loving it!

"You must ride it. Ride that black prick, Norseman!"

Saba was right. It wasn't enough merely to have the giant pole buried up his ass. He had to feel it sliding in and out! He rose upward as Saba grinned and chuckled with his massive hands squeezing the flushed ass cheeks and watching the dark meat reappear out from the distended pink ass lips.

When most of it had slid out of him, Harold reversed direction and settled back down over it. Both men emitted cries of satisfaction as the giant pole once more was buried completely within the Norseman's quivering ass lips.

More sesame oil was splashed over his round ass cheeks. Saba squeezed and rubbed the muscular globes as they rose and fell over his dark prick. Their bodies were awash in oil and sweat as Harold increased the pace of his rise and fall. Soon, he was bouncing up and down, taking the black cock to the balls, then rising up to spit most of it out.

The oily friction quickly drove them both to writhing ecstasy. Harold was first to spew, his untouched prick erupting in a spray of nut cream as he slammed his firm ass down onto Saba's slippery belly.

Saba felt the ass lips surrounding his buried prick suddenly convulse. The muscular sphincter descended into a series of spasms that milked his aching meat relentlessly as Harold shot his load all over the grass between the Nubian's spread thighs. It was too much for him. Saba erupted deep inside the Norseman's convulsing hole.

Harold hardly paused. He continued to ride the spewing prick as his nuts drained. As he had with his mouth, he drained the big Nubian dry with his asshole.

It was Saba who finally put an end to the wild ride. He lifted Harold off his prick with his big hands on his slippery buttocks, then turned him around and pulled him down into his arms. To Harold's surprise the giant Nubian pressed his lips to his and kissed him deeply.

They lay together for several hours after that, discussing their business agendas and even making bargains, such as trading the Nubian's redolent sesame oil for supple leathers and furs from the north. Both were still naked and had grown stiff again, thus the magical sesame oil was once more employed on willing holes and eager pricks.

By the time they had completed the second round, it was growing dark. Still they were reluctant to part, and so it was they made camp right there and fucked the night away, just as they had the day.

73

And even when they parted the next day, they knew it would not be the last they would see of each other. Trading partners, and friends, they would remain for the rest of their days.

COCK-LOVER
By Landon Dixon

Dixon's writing credits include many magazines and anthologies.

I'm not gay. I just like cocks – big, beautiful, long, hard, thick cocks to kiss and lick and suck and stroke and stick up my ass and get fucked by. I've got a hard-on for hard-on's. Doesn't mean I'm gay.

My lust affair with dick started when I turned eighteen and moved into the city and started watching porn on a regular basis. It started small, got big. Just like erections.

I'd be sitting in my dorm room watching pornography on my roommate's computer, and I'd find myself focusing more on those faceless, nameless, jutting cocks that were getting tugged and tongued and blown by the busty female porn stars, inserted into their every orifices. They were so huge and hunky, smooth and shiny, strong and powerful – the cocks, that is. They didn't really have faces attached to them, sometimes not even bodies, the women the stars of these sex shows. But not for me, after awhile.

I soon wanted to feel those pulsating pieces of manhood, caress them to full inflated erection, suck them to pre-cum dripping arousal, experience the wicked sensation of having those massive tubes of throbbing meat shoved whole and hard up my sensitive ass, my chute stuffed and churned until I came out my cock.

I'd jerk off to the dicks, all my attention on them, using the women only to gauge their reactions to all that buff beef, vicariously experiencing the joy they were feeling from those awesome, thrusting tools.

My roommate, Kris, caught me at it one time.

"Studying for your jack-off exam?" he cracked, my fist wrapped around my dong. The guy was back early from his seminar.

I had 'Anal Assault XXII' blazing away on the big twenty-one inch monitor, the scene where cock after magnificent cock was driven deep into the slutty star's gaping pink ass, one after another. My prick was at full mast in my hand, cum glistening at its bloated tip. There was no way I could stand down. "Y-Yeah!" I gulped. "You caught me, er, red-handed."

He grunted and tossed his textbooks onto his bed, pulled up a chair. "Anal gang-bang, huh? Yeah, that's pretty hot."

And before I even knew what was happening, he'd yanked down his fly and pulled out his cock and started stroking right next to me!

I could hardly believe my good luck; could hardly believe the fully swollen size of my roommate's dick. I'd snuck some peeks when he'd been in the shower, or changing, or sleeping in bed. But that was always unerect, much to my dismay. Now he was whole-hard, stretching up and out at least eight inches of clean-cut chocolate, hood sculpted elegance. His slender brown hand bobbed up and down, stroking his lovely appendage. As I got my own mitt back into motion, jacking right along.

But while he was grinning and staring at the X-rated action on-screen, I was grinning and staring at his hand-action, watching him caress his massive member. My own cock surged with the excitement of real, bare, beaten meat so close, my polishing hand going damp on my prong.

I had to do something more, somehow seize the opportunity presented me to further explore my encompassing cock-lust. I gulped, growled, "Ever jerk off a buddy while watching this stuff? It's kind of cool. We used to do it all the time at the private high school I went to."

I made it sound like it was no biggie. Unlike his penis. He looked over at me, and I glanced up into his brown eyes. He let go of his cock. "Sure, give it a tug, if you want."

I swallowed my cry of joy. Then I stuck out my left hand, wrapped my long, twitching fingers around his hardened, wrist-thick shaft. Fuck! It was wicked! My white hand on his ebony dong! His cock spasmed in my gripping mitt, and he grunted, thrusting it up higher. My first cock, other than my own, to jack!

I pretended to watch the monitor, shifting my hand slowly up and down Kris's erection. My face and body burned, my own cock in my other hand steeling with exhilaration. I moved my hand faster, pulling on my roomie's prong, reveling in the feel, the pulse, the size. I swirled my fingers up over his cap freestyle, twisting my wrist, really getting into it, jacking the guy with all the tricks I used to jerk myself to maximum orgasm.

"Guess one helping hand deserves another," he commented with a shrug. And reached out his right hand and grasped my dong at the base.

I bucked in my chair. Kris shunted my own hand up and off, stroking me tall and tight with his. As I tugged on his dong.

I bit my lip and sucked air through my nose, ablaze with sensation. The pretty, over-endowed man was watching the whore in the porno get fucked up the ass, thoroughly rammed and reamed. I was watching my hand on Kris' cock, polish and pull. Feeling his hand on my cock, tugging me past the point of no return.

I yanked on his dick, fisting in a fury. His cock jumped in my mitt, and he groaned, bucked. Semen burst out the tip of his mammoth, manhandled dong and spurted high up into the air, splashed down onto the floor, blast after beautiful blast. I could feel the orgasmic pump – I was responsible for it, getting another cock off. I yelped and jerked and spouted sperm out of my cock, Kris pulling it up from my balls, steaming along my pink pipe, and blasting out of my slit in soul-shivering spurts.

We never did it again, never mentioned it again, in fact. Kris picked up a girlfriend in Spanish class, and I hardly saw him around the dorm room after that. But I thought of him, the way his dark cock felt shooting in my stroking hand, every time I jacked off in our bathroom.

# # # # #

My marks, and professors, soon told me I wouldn't be long for college. So, I concentrated all my remaining time, before expulsion, on cocks. Or maybe it was my now overwhelming obsession with pricks that led to my poor grades and lack of concentration on my studies. Either way, the campus was bulging with dong. And I wanted more of it.

Not being gay, I couldn't just come out and come on to guys. But I started hanging around the men's locker and shower room at the athletic complex, that being the spot where men are most built, most underclothed, and usually most horny.

I got a membership at the gym and started pumping iron, surreptitiously pumping my prick in the communal shower room, surrounded by brawny beef. And it wasn't long before I was rewarded for all my hard work, and I was taking my next step on the road to full-blown cock worship.

I lingered in the shower one night after a basketball game. And sure enough, the men's varsity team charged in, flush from a victory, in the flesh. I crowded close to the corner wall under the last showerhead in line, covertly watching all those long-limbed, long-donged b-ballers bathe their bodies and equipment. Until I was boning out like never before in the steamy environs, and there were just three boys left with me splashing and horsing around.

I couldn't stand it any longer. The three guys were all tall, dark, and handsome and hung, their dangling dongs gleaming, streaming with moisture. I groaned and gripped my hard-on and fisted.

"Hey, this guy's got game!" someone shouted.

I turned around, clenching my jutting erection. The three dudes were looking at me, at my throttling hand, grinning. Then they hefted their own slabs of dripping meat, and the one who'd spoken before said, "C'mon over here, sweetness, and let us get in the game."

Their names were Terrance, Clement, and Odell. They beckoned at me with their cocks, the ebony pipes rising up in their soft, soapy, swirling hands. I staggered over and instinctively went down to my knees on the slick tile. And they crowded around my red head, lifting their dicks up to mouth-level.

78

This was it, something I'd been fantasizing about for months: sucking cock! And there were three of them, each one long and thick and glistening, sporting blue-black bloated caps and vein-ribboned night-shaded shafts. It was almost beyond my wildest dreams.

Terrance pushed his hood up against my lips, his dong looming large in behind. I swallowed dry despite the humid heat, sucked in some air and courage. Then I fulfilled my unstoppable craving for cock, by opening my mouth, letting Terrance slide his tremendous erection inside of me.

It was even better than I'd imagined. His meat filled my mouth, bulging my cheeks, throbbing all along my tongue. The musky scent of the man, his balls, those other cocks and balls so close, flooded my dilated nostrils and dizzy head. Shaft stretched out of my mouth as far as the crossed eyes could see. I sealed my lips tight and pushed my head forward, pulled it back, sucking the man's cock.

Terrance grunted and grabbed onto my curly hair, pumping his hips. I sucked on his dong, as he glided it back and forth in my mouth. My lips stretched obscenely, my mind blown. My hand moved up and down on my own slippery cock of its own accord, my senses occupied with the wild sensations of sucking.

Terrance pulled out, leaving me achingly, heartbreakingly empty. Clement plugged in, filling my mouth and soul once again. I dug the fingers of my free hand into one of his muscled thighs, bobbing my head earnestly, urgently, blowing his cock. He was just as delicious and developed as his teammate, as eager to fuck my face. Odell muscled in on the act, pushing Clement aside to stuff my mouth full of his cock.

My own prick was a numb slab of meat in my stroking hand, harder than it's ever been. My head spun, body bathed in hot water and hot sweat, on fire. I sucked Odell's deep-purple cock deep as I could go without gagging, held it there in the cauldron of my mouth, then pulled back with a gush of air and backwash. The guy grunted and gripped my ears, fucked my face. His hood bounced off the back of my throat, penis piling up in my mouth.

They closed ranks around me. I sucked quick and tight on one cock, sacrificing my own cock to grab onto and stroke the other pair of pricks. Then I blew slow and sensuous on another dong, pulling hard with my hands on the unmouthed dicks.

They tried to stuff two cocks inside of me, going hip to hip, prick to prick. Then three. I mouthed two caps, three, stacking them up and cramming my mouth full. There just wasn't room for them all, though, and I damned my Creator for giving me such a small sucking head-hole.

I went back to one at time – blowing; two at a time – jacking.

Terrance was the first to go off, christen my virgin mouth with sperm. He grunted and jerked and slapped the top of my bobbing head, his pipe surging in my sucking mouth, spurting. Hot, salty semen splashed against the back of my throat, filled my mouth. I swallowed, happily, joyously, frantically. Because Odell was already going off in my tugging hand, and I didn't want to miss a drop.

I spat out Terrance's spent hose and plunged Odell's ruptured pipe into my mouth. He creamed me, shooting straight down my throat so I hardly had to swallow at all. He came for what seemed like forever, endlessly. I milked his cock with my mouth and his balls with my hand for every drop of goo he could give me. Then I pulled him out and stuck Clement in.

The guy cried out and came, inspired by his teammates and my teamwork. His cock spasmed and sprayed, filling my mouth with more creamy goodness, again and again and again. I'd tasted my own sperm before, of course, but never another cock's. I couldn't get enough, my lust for dick gone insatiable.

# # # # #

As expected, I was booted out of college by the end of the first term. So, I had to get a job in the real world, find me some dong outside the ivy-clad confines of the ivory tower.

A gay co-worker at the burger joint put me onto a place: the men's restroom at a certain city park. Apparently, it was a gathering place for anonymous sex. I didn't want any part of the gaiety, of course, but I did want to feel a long, hard cock up my ass, fucking me, spunking me. It was the next lustful progression on my passionate path of prick.

My workmate wasn't kidding; the restroom was swarming with horn dogs sniffing for a hot, tight hole to call home. I'd just started jacking off at the urinal, when three men swarmed out of the stalls and the guy at the sink hustled over.

"Looking for some action?" he crooned, a slender, silky brunette with gleaming white teeth.

"I'm looking for cock – up the ass," I stated boldly on buckling legs.

He grinned. The men in behind guffawed.

They bent me over a sink and pulled my jeans down. I wasn't wearing any underwear. I felt the brunette's hand touch lightly down on my left buttock, his fingers swirl over my skin, saw him greasing his nine-inch flesh-pole in the mirror using his other hand.

'Holy shit!' I thought, this is really happening. I'm going to get that huge prick shoved up my ass, get my anus churned, my bowels splashed with semen.

"God, bring it on!" I cried out loud, gripping the sink so hard my fingers almost turned porcelain.

I was so keyed-up I barely felt the guy lube my crack, my pucker. But then I did feel something, for the first time ever: a cockhead squishing up against my virgin starfish. I clung to the sink, shaking all over.

The heat built, the tension towering upwards, that soft, meaty cockhead pushing for entry. Then it popped through, into my anus! I groaned, dizzy with feeling. The guy rotated his hood all around my ass-ring, breaking me in. Then he thrust forward, sending shaft shooting into my tunnel, busting my anal cherry in a rush.

It was fantastic! A strange, ultra-erotic, stuffed-full, bloated sensation that wiped my mind clean, left me gasping, my body

81

brimming, impaled on the end of a cock. I felt shaven balls press against my quivering buttocks, and I knew I'd never be the same man again.

The guy pistoned my ass, blazing a red-hot anal trail for the other three men. Dick after dick after dick split my cheeks and plunged my rump, pumped back and forth, in and out. I burned with an almost surreal heat, up on my toes and craning my bugged-out eyes in the mirror to try to see those beautiful black and brown and tan and pink cocks pounding into my rectum. I swelled with sensation and semen.

"Can you take two at once, baby!?" the brunette hissed in my ear, rocking me with his cock.

"I can take any amount of prong you can give me!" I rasped back, reveling in the ramming of his cock far up my ass.

One of the guys lay down on his back on the tiled floor, and I stretched out on top of him, on my back. He shoved his dark cap into my stretched ring, thrust up the rest of his gleaming black shaft into my hot-pink butt tunnel.

I groaned, watching the brunette grip his handsome hammer and crouch down, feeling him squeeze his shiny hood into my asshole, alongside of the other man's cock. He got the bulb in, stuffed more cock in. It felt like I was being torn in two; it felt wicked! The guy slowly submerged his entire shaft in my bloated bum, and I had two cocks lodged up my ass.

They pumped, fucking my butt together with their sliding pricks. As the other two men kneeled down at my head and fed their dicks into my gaping mouth.

It was too wild to last. The black man bucked under me, sprayed sizzling semen against my bowels. Quickly followed by the brunette, bathing my anus with more sperm. I shuddered with delight, swallowing spurting, superheated cum at the other end from a pair of equally spasming cocks, drinking it down.

# # # # #

Cocks. They're all I think about. Those powerful, pulsating, penetrating groin-appendages that look so lovely up-close, feel so wonderful in the mouth and the hand and up the ass.

I'm not gay. I just love penises, can't get enough of them. If women were so blessed, I'd be on them in a second, too. But since they aren't, I'm stuck with the guys. Stuck like a cock-happy pig.

SAUNSATIONAL
By Landon Dixon

I was sitting all by myself in the sauna. The heat was turned up high, the steam thick and wet. I was wearing just a white towel around my slim hips, and I had a hand burrowed down in the towel, softly, languidly stroking my hard, pulsating cock. A strenuous late-night session on the weights had left me feeling drained and fulfilled, glowing and aroused.

The door popped open, and a man intruded on my reverie.

I jerked my hand out of the towel and flung it up to my red hair, shakily ran it through. "H-Hi," I said, watching the man step up onto the third tier of cedar benches opposite me.

"Hi yourself," he responded, his voice rich and deep. He leaned back against the cedar-paneled wall and let out a sigh. "Feels good, huh?"

"Yeah ... sure does."

He was twice my young age, built twice as big. He was wearing a white towel, too, and nothing else, his huge, black, muscular upper body mushrooming up out of the skimpy tight towel, dark, thick-muscled legs pouring out from the bottom. He was shaved smooth all over like a bodybuilder, pumped up pecs and arms and thighs trained almost as ripped as one. His ebony skin gleamed with perspiration.

I felt my cock restiffen under my towel.

"Haven't seen you around before," he rumbled, looking at me.

"No! This is my first time." And I wasn't just talking about working out at the gym.

"You'll like it. Good people here. I come all the time." He grinned, teeth flashing white. "Mind if I ditch the towel?" His brown eyes twinkled through the mist.

I gulped, staring at his big, beautiful, glistening body and high-planed, handsome face. "Um, no ... not at all. Go right ..."

He arched his butt off the bench and pulled the towel away.

My tongue and eyeballs hit the tiled floor at the same time.

His cock was large and thick and vein-corded, a mahogany log even unerect. It was dark as night and just as dangerous, capped at the tip. I licked my parched lips, feeling my own cock surge, my body swell with shimmering heat.

I felt heavy, heady, as if I was in a trance, the steamy warmth and stunning sight of that naked, muscle-bound and cock-dangling man making me delightfully dizzy. I'd never been in the bare presence of such awesome, overpowering masculinity before.

"Ah, that's the stuff," he growled, shifting around on the bench, setting his black mamba to wagging between his legs. "Name's Troy, by the way." He stuck out his hand.

I was too far away to accept his greeting. I couldn't connect with the man without getting up and going over. I had to connect. I got up and went over, drawn like gravity, compelled.

I stumbled down my tier and staggered up his. My towel slipped off my hips and I grabbed at it, just as I grabbed onto Troy's big, welcoming hand. "Cody!" I yelped. He pulled me up onto his bench, his hand warm and firm and guiding, engulfing my pale little hand. I plopped down next to him, thin and white and young, a boy among man.

"Nice to meet you, Cody." He pointed a thick finger at my left pec, the lighter underside of the soft, rounded digit tip poking my pink nipple. "Looks like you got some development going on there."

I jerked, Goosebumps burning across my sallow chest at the touch of the he-man. "Th-Thanks!"

He closed his eyes and leaned his head back against the wall, spreading his legs wider apart. His huge shoulder brushed up against my puny shoulder, making me shiver. Making me boldly say, "Uh, you've got some great chest development, yourself. Can I feel it?" The last set of words spilled out of my mouth along with a string of saliva.

Troy opened his eyes and smiled at me. "Sure. Go to town." He flexed his pecs, making the dark mounds with the even darker tips dance right before my staring green eyes.

"I'm just, you know ... I'd, uh, like to get as big as you ... one day. So ..."

He pulled my left hand out of the wood and planted it on the muscle – his right pec. I grinned, giddy, feeling the clenched mass pop under my palm. I spread my fingers wide, stretching them out over his nipple. I squeezed, brushed my fingertips back and forth.

Troy grunted and closed his eyes again, shifted his feet, setting his hanging dong in motion again.

I stared down at his cock. It appeared to be lengthening, thickening. I clutched his pec, strummed the ripe rigid nipple with my fingers, hardly believing what was happening. His cock was definitely rising, engorging, spearing up and out!

I swallowed hard, and my throat cracked dry despite the one-hundred-ten percent humidity. I shifted around and threw my right hand onto Troy's left pec, gripping that mass of muscle and tissue and jutting nipple. "Y-Yeah, you really got it going, all right!" I garbled, groping the man's bouncing pecs, gazing at his surging dong. It was sticking straight out from his shaven loins, powerful and gleaming as the rest of the muscleman.

He murmured, "Take a taste, if you want."

My pale red lips trembled like my lily-white hands on his ebony chest. There was no doubting his intent, hiding his interest. Steam gushed out of my ears, and my face flushed red as my hair. It was happening – I was pushing my head forward, sticking my tongue out, tasting the hard, rubbery, licorice texture of his man-nipple.

We both jerked with the wicked warm and wet impact.

I anxiously swirled my pink tongue around and around Troy's dark nipple, making it shine, swell even further, nervously looking up into Troy's heavy-lidded, liquid-brown eyes. He softly smiled, popping his pec under my tongue. I flowered my lips and flowed them right over the straining bud, sealed them around his nipple and urgently sucked.

A tremor ran through his big body. I nursed like a hungry infant, sucking hard and tight on the man's nipple, squeezing his pecs. I yanked my head back, plunged it over, engulfing and consuming his other equally flared nipple and tugging on it.

I thought I'd melt. My face and body were on fire. Troy cupped the back of my head with a huge hand and pulled me back, gazing into my glassy eyes. "How 'bout helping me out with that new development you created?" His eyes rolled downward.

My orbs followed, down his rock-ribbed stomach to his granite-hard cock. His dong was standing up almost straight into the air, twelve inches of towering manhood. "Yes, please!"

He helped my head down. I pulled my fingers out of his chest and laced them around his cock, gripping his dick top and bottom like I'd been charming snakes all my sexual life.

"Yeah!" Troy grunted, thrusting his dong upwards between my damp little palms. It passionately throbbed in my grasping paws.

I bent over the enormous erection, staring into the blue-black bloated cap, riding my hands up and down. I was stroking, pumping the man's cock, righteously feeling the thick, pulsating, vein-ribboned length of dark meat. It was incredible, wickedly intimate. My knuckles blazed white on the beating black dong.

Troy pushed my head further down. My lips kissed up against his gaping slit. I kissed his slit, licked it, opened my mouth up wide and took his knob right inside.

I was as shocked as anyone.

"That's the stuff!" Troy groaned, shooting more massive cock into my mouth.

I couldn't see, couldn't think clearly, the steam and lust clouding my eyes and head like the man's dick was crowding my mouth. I bent my neck down at his urging, inhaling more of his pipe. It pulsed powerfully in my mouth, thundering like the blood in my ears, the beefy hood bumping up against the back of my throat. My lips stretched obscenely, my face crammed with cock, my own prick a steel rod tenting my towel.

"Suck it!" Troy bass lined.

I sucked his huge member, vaccing tight and drooling, Troy helping me bob my head up and down. I only gagged a little, pulling hard on his meat with my mouth. My nostrils flared like bellows, sweat pouring off my forehead and down onto Troy's big balls. His hips picked up the pace, pumping his cock into me, so I could go deeper, more depraved.

"How 'bout I fuck you? Workout that ass of yours?"

A tingle shot through my chute. I'd never been fucked by a man before, except in innumerable fantasies, of course. I'd never sucked a man's cock or tasted his cum before, either; but that's exactly, amazingly what I was doing – tasting a spurt of salty pre-cum from the dong I was excitedly sucking.

Troy pulled my head up. His cock slid out of my mouth, leaving me gapingly empty. It stood tall between his thighs, spit-slickened and leaking pre-cum thanks to yours truly. Troy helped swing me around, so that I ended up in his lap, sitting astride his muscular thighs in front of his jutting hammer.

My towel was lost in the erotic transfer. My own cock pronged up straight and hard and throbbing pink, right next to Troy's deep-dark dong. He gripped the pair together in his big, warm hand and pumped.

I almost shot up into the air with the sensual impact. But I managed to grab onto Troy's cinder-block shoulders just in time. I stared dazedly into his brown eyes, feeling every torrid inch of his erection pinned against my erection, our cocks burning together, melding with the pump of his hand. It was the most exquisite sensation I'd ever experienced — up to that point.

"Nice pubic muscle," Troy breathed in my face.

Then he kissed me, his plush lips splashing into mine, his brilliant pink tongue shooting into my open mouth. I feebly tried to tongue him back, but his thick, swirling, wet licker easily overpowered mine. So I just hung on and let him thrash around inside my mouth, as he churned our cocks together faster and faster.

"Oh ... Troy! I'm going to ... I'm going to ...!" I gasped, the superheated sexual situation too much for a rank amateur like myself. The guy had too much experience, too much equipment for me to compete at his level.

He immediately snapped his tongue out of my mouth and whipped his hand off our pressed cocks. "Not yet, Cody! I've got to work out that cute little ass of yours yet, remember?"

A small bottle of lube magically appeared (had he planned this all along?). I didn't even think it was necessary with all of the sweat and steam, but Troy knew best, knew just how big he was, and felt. I watched him grease his nightstick. Then he hooked an arm around my waist and lifted me up and slid a blunt finger in between my quivering white butt cheeks, rubbed my frightened starfish slick.

"Ready?" he asked.

My mouth opened and closed as if I was about to be gaffed.

Troy gripped his cock, pushed the cap up between my cheeks and against my pucker. I hung suspended on the beefy tip of his spear, not breathing. Then my butt ring buckled under the tremendous pressure, flowered. Troy's hood squished into my chute, bulging my anus.

I groaned, shaking wildly. He gripped my thin waist with both of his big hands and pressed me down, onto his black spike. Shaft glided into my ass, bloating it, stuffing me, inches and inches and inches of thick-veined, over-engorged manhood.

My rippling bum touched down on his clenched thighs. His cock was buried up my ass. It felt like that dong would come right out my throat it was cramming me so full. The sensations were strange and wicked and wonderful. I was electrified like never before with that cable coursing up my butt, making me blaze.

Troy painted my parted lips with his tongue, slowly lifting me up, down on his pile-driver. I clung to his shoulders, barely able to breathe, to comprehend, a mass of flaming raw nervy joy. He thrust his hips in rhythm to his lifting, churning my chute with his cock.

My internal temperature raged inferno, the smooth pumping action turning me incendiary. My own cock bounced right along, stiff as a frozen rope in that sexual steam bath.

Troy moved faster, stroking long and hard into my anus. I blinked my eyes for the first time in minutes, flung a sheet of sweat off my face with a toss of my head. I could see clearly now, feel everything. A man was fucking my virgin ass; he'd popped my anal cherry and now was drilling me deep as a dong could go. I helped him, bounding up and down in his lap, riding his thrusting cock.

He grinned, his teeth gritted together, face shining with perspiration, fierce with lust. I kissed him, tongued sweat off his upper lip and chin, impaling myself on his charcoal stake.

He thrust faster, higher, ecstasy egging us on. A man fucking another man up the ass – the most natural and beautiful workout there is. The wooden bench creaked and our tightened flesh cracked together, our breath coming in gasps.

"Fuck, Cody! I'm gonna..."

"Me, too!"

He hammered up my chute in a frenzy, tossing me into the air. My wildly flapping cock erupted, spouting sizzling semen all over Troy's clenched pecs and abs. I cried pure bliss, riding the man's ram-rod to heaven. As he howled and bucked, blasted steaming sperm up my butt.

I was coming, a man was coming inside me; my wildest dreams coming true. It went on and on, my cock spurting forever, his cock shooting me full of an ecstasy I'd never known existed before.

I probably lost ten pounds off my slender frame in that cauldron of a sauna, along with my innocence. And then I almost lost my mind, when I saw Troy leaving the gym with a woman, whom he introduced as his wife.

"Cody and I are workout buddies, Rachel," he explained to the statuesque redhead. Then he grinned at me. "Same time, same place on Wednesday ... buddy?"

My head bobbed up and down as it had in the gorgeous guy's lap.

I couldn't wait for another sauna session with Troy, so he could develop me further as a man.

HEAVENLY HELL WEEK
By Landon Dixon

It was hell week, and all heaven was breaking loose. The fraternity houses ringing the campus were putting their pledges through the final five days of rigorous loyalty and honor testing before true initiation. And Bryant Barnes was right in the middle of the mayhem.

The tall, slim, dark-skinned African-American loved this time of year – pledge season – best of all. There was nothing to compare to it off-campus. All the eager young men doing whatever it took to become part of a fraternity, undergoing the trials and tribulations and exultations that were all a part of their journey to true manhood. Academics were put on hold; action was the name of the game.

Bryant's plush, purple lips parted in a grin, revealing strong, sparkling white teeth, as he gripped the iron handrail and climbed the wooden steps up to the oldest fraternity on campus, staring at the large, red Greek letters that adorned the front of the 19th century mansion, a beacon of welcome to all men of his bent.

Two fraternity brothers and six pledges were waiting for him in the foyer of the house when he pushed through the big oaken doors. "About time you got back from the beer run, pledge!" Conrad barked. "Get down on your hands and knees! There's keyholing to be done!"

Bryant dropped the beer cases on a table next to the door then dropped to his hands and knees on the polished floor. The six pledges immediately followed suit, diving to the floor, anxious to obey.

Conrad inspected them from above. He was a big, muscular, ivory-skinned twenty-two year-old with glossy black hair and a square, chiseled face, bright blue eyes. The brother with him was Luis, a small, wiry guy the same age as Conrad. Luis was copper-skinned, brown-eyed, his face smooth and delicate, lips lush and erotic. He watched Conrad look over the seven young men on all-fours, his eyes gleaming with a deep, abiding passion.

"Okay, up the stairs," Conrad ordered. "You're going to clean the keyholes on the brothers' bedroom doors. No peeking inside, either," he added, winking at Luis.

Bryant quickly scrambled to the lead of the pack, began crawling up the blue-carpeted stairs on his hands and knees, the others rapidly following after him. The brothers brought up the rear, appreciating the view of seven clenching, clutching, twitching sets of buttocks tightly encased in jeans and khakis. They herded the pledges up the stairs and onto the second floor landing, down the hall to the first door.

The house being so old, the dark wooden bedroom doors all had old-fashioned keyholes, with working locks. Conrad and Luis ranged the seven pledges out down the long hallway, assigning a bedroom door to each of them. The pledges kneed into position in front of the doors, then rose up onto their haunches, staring at the keyholes, compliantly awaiting further instructions.

Conrad glanced at Luis, back at the kneeling young men. "Well, start cleaning those keyholes! What are you waiting for?"

Bryant looked up at the man, quizzical as the rest of the bunch. "Uh, what are we supposed to clean the keyholes with?" he asked as politely as possible.

Luis snorted.

Conrad stated, "With your tongues, of course."

Bryant gulped. "Oh." Then he stuck out his long, brilliant-pink tongue and rimmed the brass keyhole fixture.

The other pledges looked at him, then rushed to take up their task with their tongues. Six lickers shot out and began swirling brass, squirming inside and around keyholes.

"Get in there deep!" Conrad exhorted, strutting up and down the hallway. "I want to see that brass shine inside and out."

Bryant washed his thick tongue all over the fixture, making it gleam. Then he shaped his pink sticker into a blade, jabbed it inside the

94

large keyhole. And felt something warm and soft on the end of his tongue.

He jerked his head back, down, went eye-level with the opening in the door. He stared into what appeared to be a fraternity brother's spread ass on the other side of the door.

"See something you like, pledge?" Luis said, walking up behind Bryant.

Bryant popped his head back up, swiveled it around. And stared into the taut, tawny twin cheeks of Luis's bare ass.

The brother's pants were gone, just his shoes and socks and shirt remained. He reached back and grasped his copper buttocks, spread them, revealing his darker-hued pucker. "Well, keep cleaning."

The other pledges had all met fraternity asses through their designated keyholes, as well. Now they turned their heads and gaped at Bryant, as the young man kneed around and planted his tongue in between Luis's open cheeks, licked up the brother's smooth-shaven crack.

Luis groaned and quivered. The pledges gulped and trembled.

Conrad was sans pants, too. His buttocks were huge and round and creamy-white, pink cock dangling between his muscular legs. He strode up to the junction of Bryant's tongue and Luis's ass, inspected the lickmanship. "Good work, pledge," he allowed, watching Bryant drag his widened tongue up and down Luis's crack, to Luis's panting satisfaction. "The rest of you, you've seen how it's done. Now back to work."

The pledges went back to cleaning the keyholes, touching, teasing the brothers' brown eyes on the other sides of the doors. Their keyholing was only interrupted when Conrad or Luis presented them with an ass up-close and personal. Then they earnestly licked that brother's crack, wet-stroking sensitive bum cleavage, the better performers diving deep between the brothers' legs and swabbing perineum and crack all the way up to tailbone, again and again.

After enthusiastically licking Luis's ass, Bryant happily went back to keyholing. He shoved and writhed his tongue as deep as it would go into the keyhole, to taste as much of the brother's ass on the other side that he could. Until Conrad cleared his throat right next to the kneeling man, and Bryant yanked two inches of twisted tongue out of the keyhole, reformed it flat, and applied it in wide, sweeping strokes to Conrad's deep, tender butt cleavage.

They weren't allowed to touch, just lap. But that was more than good enough for Bryant. He slurped quick, then slow, really dragging Conrad's crack in long, sensuous, budded licks. Then he paused at the man's engorged pucker, and painted the wrinkled rim of manhole with his twirling tongue.

Conrad jumped and grunted, gyrated his ass on Bryant's tongue. As Bryant stuck the hardened pink spear right into Conrad's open butthole and squished it around inside the brother's anus.

The other pledges were thus encouraged to go as deep and dirty as they could, too. Luis felt the erotic benefits, a pledge jabbing away at his chute with bladed tongue.

Bryant flat-out fucked Conrad's trembling ass with his tongue, drilling hard and deep, setting Conrad's cock to jumping on the other side. Until the man himself had to jump forward, off Bryant's wicked tongue.

The keyholing continued up and down the line, until holes on doors and brothers truly did shine.

# # # # #

There was a small party in the large fraternity house living room after the keyholing chores had been completed. Half the brothers were there, twelve men, and all of the seven pledges. The pledges were required to do the serving – crawling back and forth on their knees between the kitchen and living room balancing cans of beer and bowls of chips on their heads.

"Now, don't drop anything," Conrad warned the kneeling young men in the kitchen.

"Yeah, that'll really suck," Luis said, grinning along with his brother.

The two men outfitted the pledges with a beer can each on their heads and then led them from the kitchen, down the hall, into the living room. The brothers were all standing around waiting, with no pants on, just like Conrad and Luis.

The pledges halted as a body, staring at the group of half-naked men. The brothers' cocks jutted out from their loins, long and hard and thick. All of the men were well-built where it counted most.

"Well, come on, pledges!" Conrad barked from behind. "Start servicing."

Bryant took the initiative for the group once again, marching forward on his knees with the beer can on his head. Marching, perhaps, too aggressively. His right knee hit a bump in the blue carpet and the beer can tumbled off the back of his head.

"That sucks," commented the brother who Bryant was beer-bound for. His name was Marvis, a chocolate-hued man of medium height and weight, with glasses and short-cropped hair, an enormous, pitch-black dong. Marvis hefted his meat, gestured at Bryant with it.

Bryant looked back at Conrad, his eyes showing their whites, all of the other pledges' eyes gone wide, as well. Conrad nodded.

Bryant turned his head back around and crawled forward on his knees, up to Marvis's pointing cock. Marvis pried Bryant's lush lips open with his bloated cap, fed vein-swollen shaft into Bryant's hot, wet, red mouth, along moistened pink tongue. He didn't stop until he hit the back of Bryant's throat.

Bryant sealed his lips around the huge dong filling his face. Marvis pumped his hips, fucking Bryant's mouth.

"Beer me or blow me!" the rest of the brothers chimed as one.

Pledges moved shakily forward on their knees. Some made it to a brother without spilling their precious cargo. Some didn't. Those who didn't had their lips stretched and mouths punished with a fully-erect, pulsating cock, plowing inside them and pumping. Bryant did more than just take the delicious donging to the tonsils, however. Exhilarated by the taste, the feel, the pulsing power of all that meat in his mouth, the musky scent of Marvis's pube-dotted balls, Bryant excitedly bobbed his head back and forth in rhythm to Marvis's thrusting, sucking on the man's pumping pipe. Intimately and intensely servicing the brother.

Marvis had to jerk his hips back, pop his slathered cock out of Bryant's sweet vaccing mouth, before he prematurely ended the party for himself.

Bryant kneed back and forth between the kitchen and living room, along with the other pledges, a steady, crawling line of young, open-mouthed men. Bryant seldom made it all the way with his load of chips or beer. He caught Luis's lengthy cock in his mouth for his carelessness, sucked heavy and heady on Conrad's smooth-shafted, wrist-thick dong as a result of his clumsiness.

The brothers didn't fully let loose, though. That was saved for the basement cleaning and reaming that evening.

# # # # #

All twenty-five brothers showed up for the get-together in the basement of the frat house. None of them was wearing pants, just like at the afternoon party. Only now, the seven pledges weren't wearing pants, or any other stitch of clothing for that matter.

Conrad explained, "This is the final test before initiation. You're under no obligation to participate. But for those who do – willing and ably – we'll know for sure that those are the types of men we're looking for."

Bryant was the first to rip off his shirt and pants, kick off his shoes, skin down his shorts. His ebony body gleamed under the fluorescent lights, smooth and lithe and luscious, blue-black cock rising up from his shaven loins with excitement. He had been issued the first toothbrush and shot glass full of soapy water, the first exhortation to begin scrubbing the tiled basement floor.

The other pledges had all followed suit, right down to their birthday suits. The brothers gripped their cocks and stroked, staring down at the seven stuck-up, jiggling asses of the pledges scrubbing at the floor.

Bryant felt a mist hit his upraised bottom, a pair of fingers slip in between his tightened cheeks to rub the lube in. He quivered, scraping at a tile with his clenched toothbrush. And then something bulbous and beefy parted his dusky seat cushions, pressed up against his tingling manhole.

He lifted his head from the floor and looked back. Marvis grinned back at him, blindingly. The brother was squatted in behind, the tip of his dark meat buried in Bryant's buttocks. He gripped the young man's waist and thrust his hips forward. Bryant felt slickened cap squish through his resisting ring, lodge in his ass; and then he experienced the sensational, shimmering rush of rock-hard erection sliding into his chute, bloating his butt and bursting his mind.

Bryant dropped the toothbrush and clawed at the tiles. The gliding, gilding plunge of cock into his ass was awesome, electrifying. He thought the big brother would ball right out his mouth, the dong was so huge and fulfilling. But balls pressed up against his buttocks, halting the heady descent of dick. Bryant and Marvis gasped for air, the two men joined in wicked fraternity.

The other pledges were getting their asses stuffed with cocks. Groaning and grunting filled the heated air. But Bryant could only concentrate on one ass and one cock at a time – the pipe plugging his butt. It shifted, pulling back, leaving gaping emptiness behind; then bulled forward again, pushing in utter fulfillment. As Marvis fucked Bryant's ass.

Bryant pushed back, meeting the meaty man's thrusts, convulsing his butt muscles so that he sucked on the shunting cock. They moved faster and faster, as one, their groans of delight, the glorious smacking of their flesh, the velvety, searing friction of cock stoking chute, blotting out their minds to everything else.

Marvis pounded into Bryant's bounding butt. Then jerked back and out just in time. Another cock instantly stuck Bryant's ass, tunneling and torquing his chute. As Marvis staggered off to hit and hammer another pledge's sweet ass.

One cock after another barged into and banged Bryant, every brother taking a shot at every pledge. Until Bryant had actually dug up a tile from the floor, his burning body rocking to and fro with the wild free-for-all fucking, his brain jarred loose by the brutal and beautiful pounding he was taking and loving. His anus reamed raw as his emotions, his cock jutting out cum-hard and jerking in rhythm to the anal-assaults. He was ready to blow, explode into a thousand specks of semen all over the basement.

"Good work, 'pledge'!" Conrad grunted, stuffing his shiny pink dong into Bryant's gaping wide asshole. "You showed the real pledges the way. Now you'll get your just reward."

The brother grabbed onto Bryant's shoulders and pulled him upwards on his knees. He kissed, licked, bit into Bryant's neck, tongued his ears, Bryant's outstretched and flailing tongue, as he pistoned cock into Bryant's ass. And then he dropped a hand down Bryant's sweat-slickened, heaving chest and grabbed onto the man's onyx cock, pumped it to the pace of the frantic fucking.

Bryant jerked up against Conrad, bellowed. Superheated orgasm exploded inside him. His ass clamped Conrad's cock, semen spraying out of his hand-jacked erection again and again and again. He hardly felt the sizzling spurts of joy from Conrad's erupting cock in his anus, the mind-blowing bliss of total release carrying him away.

# # # # #

Bryant walked off the college campus with a noticeable gait to his carriage and a smile on his lips. He wasn't even a student, let alone a member of a fraternity. But he'd be back next year to participate in another heavenly hell week, a ringer brought in to get pledges to fully engage with their brothers. It worked wickedly well for all parties concerned.

THIS SIDE OF UNBEARABLE
By R. W. Clinger

R. W. Clinger resides in Pittsburgh. He writes for STARbooks Press.
Black dudes are a weakness for his white skin. R. W. can be reached by
e-mail at rwclinger@verizon.net or through his website
www.rwclinger.com.

ONE – BACHELOR NUMBER THREE

The instructions were quite simple to follow at The Brat House, a gay-friendly community center, regarding Friday night's Three-Minute Dating Gig:

Fifteen, two-person tables were placed in a circle. Seated on the right side of each table was a single bachelor. All fifteen of those men were of various cultures, skin tones, widths, builds, smiles, and whatnots. All were handsome or puppy dog cute in their own ways. And all were over twenty-one years old.

Standing at the front of the room were fifteen more men, which included Quiver, Jason, and me. My friends coaxed me to attend the function, even though I wasn't looking for a date, boyfriend, and another guy to pal around with, since I probably had one too many on hand. Jokingly, Quiver and Jason said that if I didn't attend the Three-Minute Dating Gig they wouldn't be my friends anymore. Little coaxing worked, and I was ready for whatever was about to happen.

No, I had never done speed dating before, but what the hell, right? What did I really have to lose? Quiver said he ended up with a few boyfriends from the event. And Jason confessed that he had landed some great one-night stands. God only knew what I would get out of the deal.

Tina, a drag queen who looked exactly like Taylor Swift, said to the men surrounding me, "Gentlemen and Queens, find a seat, darlings. Let's begin. You have three minutes to learn everything you can about the sexy and bitchy bachelors in front of you. I do hope each of you find your Mr. Right."

Quiver discovered a seat across from a professor-looking redhead.

Jason ended up across from a bulky, Italian wrestler.

I chose a blue-eyed doll with thick brown hair, dimples, and a pretty boy smile.

Tina informed, "Begin, guys!"

Blue eyes took my white-boy sexy in from head to chest across from him: pale white skin, fauxhawk-styled bleached blond hair, thin build, five-ten frame, one-hundred-sixty pounds, pinkish lips, fall-into green eyes. He asked, "How old are you?"

"Twenty-three." I asked, "How old are you?'

"Twenty-one … You a top or bottom?"

The question caught me off guard, but I answered it anyway, "Bottom … What about you?"

"Bottom."

"That could be a problem."

He nodded. "I guess so. What do you do for your rent money?"

"Professional house-sitter. I have my own business."

"Really?" Blue Eyes raised his eyebrows and pursed his lips.

"You don't believe me?"

He shook his head. "Not particularly."

I said, "We have no chemistry, do we?" Plus, he was far too white for my taste in the men I regularly dated.

"You haven't made my dick hard. Is that what you mean?"

"It's exactly what I mean," I replied, sat back in my chair, rolled my eyes, and waited for Tina to ring a bell, which would allow me to move onto the next bachelor.

# # # # #

Bachelor number two was hot to the nth degree: Latino-perfect, six-five structure, two-hundred-forty pounds of all muscle, twinkling almost-purple eyes, scruff on his cheeks and chin, coat of arms tattoo on his right bicep, chest the size of an Army tank, broken nose that was sexy as hell.

I sat across from his hulking frame and asked, "What's your name?"

He tapped his nametag sticker and said, "Tonto."

"Honestly?"

"For real. It's on my birth certificate."

"My name is Schultz ... Adam Schultz."

"You Jewish?"

"One-hundred percent. Do you like Jews?"

"You're cut, right?"

I nodded. "Why, do you prefer uncut?"

He shook his head. "You play sports, Schultz?"

"Nope. I house-sit. What do you do?"

"Professional football player."

"For the Kingstons?"

He nodded, which was a little too much head-bobbing for me.

"What position?"

"What position do you want me to play?"

"Tight-end." I said. Why not? I didn't want to be a prude and not play with him.

"Too cliché. Pick another position."

"Overtop me?" I asked, playing easy, and smiling from ear to ear in the process.

"I like you, Schultz … and your cut shaft."

"My eight-inch cut shaft," I corrected. "How big is your wanker?"

"Wanker?" he inquired, raising an eyebrow with a rather boyishly rugged smile on his handsome face.

"Your dick," I corrected. "How long is your dick?"

"Let's just say I can tickle the back of your throat when I fuck you from behind."

"Wow, that's pretty long."

Tina rang the bell, and my short date with Tonto ended.

Before I rose from his table, he said, "I'll keep you in mind, Schultz. You were kind of fun. Besides, who doesn't like a sexy house-sitter?"

"Just imagine how I am in bed," I provided, sauntered to the next table and bachelor number three.

# # # # #

Kintano Kind. That was the singlelite's name. His looks were unbearably handsome, and everything I liked in a man: chocolate-colored skin, amber eyes, thin eyebrows, deep cleft in the chin, onyx-colored buzz cut, six-two frame, one-hundred-ninety pounds of all muscle, thick neck, thick shoulders, GQ smile.

"Kintano Kind," he said, shaking my hand.

"Adam Schultz."

I told him what I did for a living, how old I was, and that I rather liked dark-skinned men.

He said he was twenty-nine years old, worked with autistic children, had a degree in social health from Temple, and was the youngest of seven brothers.

"Jesus, that's a lot of testosterone, Kintano."

He laughed. "You have any siblings?"

I shook my head.

"What are your hobbies?"

"Running. Planning trips. Eating southern food. Sleeping around with big black studs."

"I'm from the south," he said.

"Which state?"

"Georgia."

"Atlanta?"

He nodded.

"You don't look gay."

"I like white dick, if that's what you're getting at," he said, and chuckled thereafter.

"I'm rather fond of black dick," I admitted.

He winked at me in a seductive manner.

"You're unbearably cute."

"And you're my type," he said, grinning with a bright-white smile.

"You work out," I commented.

"Three times a week. How about you?"

105

"I run about four times a week, or try to."

"You're as white as I am black."

"I have some Irish in me."

"Would you like some black in you?" he quipped, teasing me.

"Are you flirting with me?"

He raised both eyebrows, which explained interest in my question. "White on chocolate … I like that."

"How about chocolate inside white? What do you say?"

"I say we click, Adam."

"Schultz," I corrected him. "Everyone calls me Schultz."

He shook his head. "I'm calling you Adam."

I was about to say something smart to him, but Tina interfered our short romance with her bell-ringing, and I moved to the next table where bachelor number four sat and waited for our date to begin.

# # # # #

I dated all fifteen men and thought Kintano an adequate fit for me. As I pondered my short period of time with the social worker, Quiver left The Brat House and went home with his professor. Jason was pulled out of the queer-friendly community center and whisked to a different part of the city by a military man. Once alone, Kintano found me near the concession and said, "Hey, it's you again."

"Schultz," I said.

"You mean Adam," he corrected, and handed a napkin to me. "That's my cell number. Call or text me. I really want to go out with you."

"What about tonight? The night is young. What do you say?"

He shook his head and said, "No can do."

"You hiding a white boyfriend at home?"

Kintano laughed. "Not quite."

"Suit yourself," I uttered, maybe a little dismayed that he didn't want to spend a few more hours with me.

Before vanishing from my side, he moved up to me, brushed a finger along my chin, and whispered, "You're sexy as hell."

"I really don't try to be."

"You wear it well, my new friend."

Before I knew what was happening, he clutched his arms around me, pressed his hulking chest against my chest, and dabbed a kiss to my right cheek.

Truth was, I felt crushed against his massive size, but really didn't care. The outline of his cock in his denim jeans pressed against my leg. His biceps were inflated with numerous veins and aligned to my sides. His breath was minty fresh and proved he was a non-smoker.

When the hug and light kiss ended, I said, "Your skin smells like hot chocolate."

He shrugged a massive shoulder and replied, "I'll take what I can get, man. Thanks for the hug."

TWO – OPPOSITES ATTRACT

My last boyfriend was too white; I thought that all the time about him. Leonard was a Republican and seemed too old for his smooth ivory-colored skin. I think he was a bigot to tell you the truth, even if he liked to fuck guys. He hated the masses with utter joy, learned to despise my Jewish mother, and thought I was a bitch. Fortunately, Leonard was out of the picture. After two long years with the fucker, I no longer had to deal with his hate for the world. So long. Farewell, asshole.

There were other black dicks I dated in the past few years, but none of them treated me well at all. Kintano had a different approach about his nature, which I didn't find offensive. Instead, I believed him to be rather polite, caring, and interested in treating me substantially well. So that was the number one reason why I decided to text him the following night:

Adam – K, it's Schultz.

Kintano – I remember you, white chocolate. What's up, Adam?

A – Schultz. Call me Schultz.

K – I want to call you under me, but I'm a gentleman.

A – Do you want to have a drink with me tonight?

K – It depends what we're drinking.

A – What do you drink?

K – Straight Jack over ice. There's nothing better.

A – I can arrange that.

K – Where and when?

A – I'm house-sitting. 829 Soss Street. Be here at seven tonight.

K – I'll be there.

A – Sounds great.

# # # # #

The house was haunted, I swear. Things went bump in the night, and I knew that those mysterious sounds were not of two men having sex after dark. In truth, I invited Kintano over to protect me throughout the night. If I could get him to stay until dawn, maybe I wouldn't poo myself from fright.

Of course he was prompt. The black ambition carried a bottle of Jack in his right hand, wore an ear-to-ear smile on his face, and said upon entering the abode, "Who owns this masterpiece?"

"A friend of mine. His name is Adrian Hart."

"Like the porn star?"

"Same name, different color of skin."

"That's a perfect color of skin for me. You know I like white dudes." He moved up to me, nuzzled his chin to the back of my neck, darted his tongue out, and licked my flesh.

I pulled away from him and admitted, "Drinks first ... Kissing later."

"Every game has its rules, doesn't it?"

"Sometimes the rules can be fun."

Frankly, I felt that I was on this side of unbearable regarding his cocoa-colored skin. My hunger for the six-two man was nothing less than dick-rising. Of course, I sported bubbles of pre-goo inside the snug, navy blue Aussiebum at my middle. Discretely, I gave the log a push and shove to allow it to deflate, but my action was ineffective. To speak the truth, the private part only became harder, sexually agitated, and wanted nothing less than to be coveted by the man's tight palm, throat, or even his ink-hued ass – whatever it was going to take to spray my white seed over his midnight-black skin that evening.

Within the partially dark study filled with Chippendale chairs, a desk, an Elizabethan settee, and floor-to-ceiling windows around us, some gravitational pull only wanted me closer to his hulking charcoal-colored frame as we got drunk together on his gifted Jack. One shot turned into seven ... nine ... eleven, and we easily came together in a man-with-man kiss. Inseparable, his massive palms discovered my hips, and he pulled my tight tee over my head, dropping it to the walnut floor. As a masculine and queer ghost whispered something in the distance, an external autumnal wind scratched at the room's vast windows. He grazed his long and dark fingers over every muscled line on my torso. Fingertips and manicured nails brushed my puckered navel, white and shadowy abs, and both nipples. As our kiss ensued, our tongues played together. Chest to chest, we languidly felt lust-driven among the haunted souls and unquiet mansion.

Yes, I was relentlessly attracted to his soot-hued skin and hulking body. And yes, I was perfectly fine if the sociologist coveted every inch of my body with his mouth: the swollen eight-inches of crank between my legs, the nape of my muscular back, both running-constructed shoulders, and my bulbous white bottom. To have the charcoaled and cut stranger pry my rump open with his invading fingers, protruding tongue, or ten-inch shaft, was not beneath me. In fact, the thought of all three actions seemed appropriate since I was unable to prevent my skin from connecting with his. To be fucked by the found man would have only cured me of my sexually delusional state, and left the both us in a place that we could have easily called our haunted euphoria.

Unfortunately, the intimate act of his chocolate-hued body connected to my ivory-colored one was not part of the scheme for that night. No, our flesh did not go bump in the night and intimately mesh. Instead, the haunted mansion had other plans for us and spawned a new life of terror. No longer did we sport erections. Nor were our sexual drives at their relentless apexes. On the contrary, the windows within the expansive study blew open and closed around us, ghostly boy-shrieks echoed within the mansion's confines, and the hulking chandeliers flicked on/off, on/off, on/off.

During those mind-altering and spine-clenching events, Kintano and I broke apart, bolted from the room, and escaped the palatial and haunted house. How we became separated outside the devil-ridden abode was not logical. My sidekick drove away in the night, leaving me behind.

Although he had become a frightened kitten by the paranormal events in Adrian Hart's home, I still found him attractive on various levels, and desired nothing less than to have his onyx skin align with my frosty-white flesh, combining our heated bodies with incurable sex.

THREE – LET THE UNLOADING BEGIN

I did not hear from Kintano Kind for the next two weeks. Perhaps he was embarrassed regarding his scare at the Hart mansion. I was certainly aware that a man of his professional stature and brazen bulk did not take lightly to being scared shitless. No matter what had transpired at the haunted abode, I had clearly told myself that I wasn't going to hold it against him. In truth, his fleeing episode in the night was our little secret, an action and tale I had never planned to share with my closest friends, and didn't.

Serendipity transpired between us without providing a warning signal. Again, we bumped into each other at The Brat House. Between acts of an extremely gay-themed and uber-boring play called *This Side of Unbearable*, I accidentally fell into Kintano's black and hulking chest. Both of us just happened to be bolting from the gay-friendly community center, escaping the thumbs-down play. To no avail, surprising me, the bulky socialist caught me in his arms, grinned down at me, and said, "You're right where I want you to be, Adam."

"Schultz," I corrected him.

"I will never call you that," he admitted. "You're my white Jew, always."

I felt comfortable against his onyx mass, stared into his amber-colored eyes, and said, "I'm sorry about the haunted mansion thing."

"Forgotten," he admitted. "I've missed you."

He barely knew me, but whatever.

Other viewers of the badly executed play were leaving and walked around our twosome. As bodies gingerly scampered about us, he admitted, "I have an idea."

"What kind of idea is that?" I was still locked in his arms. In fact, my cheek was pressed against one of his hulking shoulders, which caused a nervous bolt of affection for his blackness to tumble within my stomach.

"I live a few blocks from here. What do you say we finish what we started at your friend's house?"

"Clarify that, Kintano."

He laughed: pearly whites and wide amber eyes lit up his handsome face. The man leaned into me, nuzzled his lips against my left ear, and said, "I want to shove my ten-inch black cock into your white ass. What do you say?"

It was my turn to laugh. Then I joked in return, "My white ass prefers twelve inches, but your black ten will just have to do."

# # # # #

His loft was on the eleventh floor of the Chamber Building and overlooked Brat Park. As I held a shot of Jack in front of his floor-to-ceiling window and stared down into the park's nightly confines (cobblestone walkways, yellow-gold lights, two coy ponds, a few fountains), I inquired, "Do you pick up white dudes down there?"

"Only when I'm really horny and need to jack out a load."

"So you're just semi-horny tonight?"

"Not quite. I have a stronger affection for you. You're quite special to me, if you want to know the truth."

I spun around from the view of the park and noticed he had already stripped his shirt off, which was on the floor near his right foot. The man sported a massive black chest with barbell-size nipples, ladder-like abs, and a curly trail of black treasure hair beneath his comma-shaped navel. His skin was chocolaty perfect, muscularly toned, and rather fine for my Jewish, white boy needs. Once my study of his unclothed chest occurred, I inquired, "Do you find me unbearable, Kintano?"

"I do," he responded, downed his Jack, decided on a second shot, and consumed the throat-burning concoction just as fast as the first.

"Why do you find me unbearable?"

"It's your blond hair, Irish-white skin, and Jewish background."

I emptied my shot glass, took the bottle of Jack away from him, drank a second shot from the bottle, handed the glass container back to him, and said, "What do you plan to do with my blond hair, Irish-white skin, and Jewish background?"

"Unload my pent desire all over you."

"How so?" I closed in on his skin, brushed my whiskey-scented lips over his right, black nipple, and quickly pulled away.

"You should stick around and find out," he replied, and grabbed the already-hard shaft that was hidden under my denim jeans, between my thick thighs, providing the mass with a hearty and dick-jolting squeeze that I rather enjoyed.

"Trust me, guy ... I'm not leaving."

"Then let the unloading begin."

FOUR – BLACK IS BETTER

I admit today, my mother would not have been proud of me that night. There I was, completely naked and pressed against Kintano Kind's floor-to-ceiling window that overlooked Brat Park and other parts of the almost-asleep city. My back was concave so my tight, white ass could be of use for his hungry service, and my palms were pressed against the sprawling window. Of course my legs were cocked open and my dick just happened to be rock-hard between my thighs. And yes, my balls sloppily hung beneath my erection, swinging left and right.

Kintano munched on my rump with pleasure: slurping ensued, oxygen was huffed, and the tip of his tepid and red tongue explored my insides. He drove his face against my end, attempted to semi-suffocate himself, pulled away, and gave my bottom a light spanking, which I truly enjoyed.

I was lost in front of him: windblown, on a plane of wanderlust, and completely entranced by his man-action. Another smack occurred to my pale orbs, and I let out a boyish whimper of delight.

Behind me, he asked, "Do you like that?"

"More than you know."

Of course I expected another hand-slap to my rear, but that didn't transpire. Instead, my eleventh floor friend darted his tongue into my hub, pulled away, and darted it inside again.

Without any control whatsoever regarding the post between my legs, a string of goo leaked out of the ivory-white shaft and hung to the floor. Aware of my pre-shoot show, the black stud behind me reached around me with his right hand, gathered the string of spew and then my dick. With the creamy drizzle on his fingers and palm he cranked the tool at my center. Of course his face was still in my ass, which provided the end-hole with persistent licks, unstoppable laps, and the occasional gnaw.

Brat Park was a blur in front of me because of Kintano's steady face-work on my hub. My forehead actually bumped against the plane of glass, which shook within its frame. Once, and only once, did I actually feel his teeth on my interior, which drove me mad. A gasp escaped my open mouth and tears ebbed at the corners of my eyes. Tap … tap … tap occurred as my head continued to meet the glass window. The sound told me that the man behind me was knocking and wanted inside my tight center. "Kintano," escaped my lips as I wavered in front of him and almost slid down the window's transparent surface. He held me up though with his left palm squashed against my hip and his right palm joined to the stiff shaft between my muscular and pale white thighs.

Eventually he pulled off and away from me, discovered some plastic in his loft, returned to my ass in just a few seconds, and proclaimed over the splay of my back, "Black is better, man. Here goes."

# # # # #

I admit his pounding was like nothing I had ever expected. The sociologist's movement was rough, wild, sporadic, and relentless. Half of me believed it clumsy but quite enjoyable. All ten inches of his black spike throttled my insides, completely pulled out, and pushed inside my crack again. Hyper bucking followed while he forcefully dug his fingers into my hips. The man's bolts were unending and felt as if they were tearing my insides to shreds. Not that I cared, though, since I desired nothing less regarding his naked company.

"It's all in the bang, man," he huffed behind me.

"Bang away, Kintano," I coached, prepared to consume his roughness, and whatever else he had to share with my white bottom.

Candidly speaking, I felt as if his cock was actually sliding into the back of my throat by way of my asshole. Ten inches of his mast slid into me, pulled out, and slid inside again. His motion was grossly forceful but manageable. And he was right, black was better, compared to the few white guys with their skinny frames who had taken an interest in my behind with their ivory and slender cocks.

Again and again, I was plunged forward, backward, forward, and backward. His stick-to-hole action was nothing less than tyrannical, but offered an endless amount of satisfaction and zeal. The black man was hefty in size, both regarding his dick's length and girth, and felt roughly euphoric inside my body. My ass, back, head, and even my legs hurt because of his ride, but that didn't stop me from enjoying his offered pleasure. Instead, I relished his ten-inch black tool and its fierce motion to the fullest. Not once was I about to stop his battering because of my sexual indulgence.

As expected, he was ready to churn out his thick and gooey load, and explained, "I'm going to burst."

"Do it," I coached, feeling like a male cheerleader in front of him.

And so it was done. Kintano yanked his beef out of my end, lost the condom somewhere in the room, and began jacking his meat up and down with both fists.

What I saw in the plane of glass in front of me was similar to the hulking and maddening ghost that I believed lived inside Adrian Hart's mansion. A reflective shadow of the black man appeared on the glass and shifted to and fro with his cock securely tucked in his right hand. One center-bolt turned into a dozen or more as the six-two structured figure attempted to find bliss. A howling sound echoed within the loft that reminded me of the familiar and nightly noises at Adrian's: unearthly grunts mixed with grinding teeth, potent gasps of fright, and a constant breathing. As the two moments in my life became similar, the man behind me explained, "Here it comes."

No, his pent load did not cover the nape of my back, ass orbs, bulky shoulders, or even my hair. Instead, his shoot spiraled against the window's glass on the left side of my head. There it hung, white and creamy clumps that stuck to the view of Brat Park. And there it started to slowly be pulled down by gravity, just as come moves, along the glass surface.

# # # # #

"I want to jack your load on me," he said, spinning me around to face him. The black god reached for my stick with both palms, wrapped his ten digits and palms around my upright flag, and began to gyrate the excess skin on my post in a speedy north and south motion.

It was not going to take me long to come, I knew. In fact, just a few strokes by the work of his thrifty hands could cause me to empty my system of its creamy freight. There, facing him, my white ass exposed to the city of Brat, my bare back and shoulders, my muscular thighs and ripped legs, all of which could be seen by the city, shivered as he jacked me off. Together we made eye contact, amber mixed with emerald, and both of us smiled. Of course I was instructed, "Fuck my hands, man," and listened to his spill.

What transpired was rather expected regarding the action between naked fags. I bucked his handy hands with skill, and he moved the pair up and down with speed on my eight-inch stick. Together, we worked in synchronized motion, enjoying our sex-fun in his loft. And together, we mixed our skin color of black and white, creating a better place for races to coexist in the world. Bigotry was replaced with man-lust between us. Racism was nonexistent. Our bond was simply two colors that blended as one; an act between us that was entirely bearable.

"Now," I confessed, feeling a zigzagged bolt of electric fire throughout my core, knowing I was about to shoot.

"Give me a show," he informed, delighted with his task and my ivory-white cock inside his butter rum-colored hands.

And a show it was, I surmised. My body heaved forward and exploded gooey seed all over his chest. White strings of sap decorated his black pecs and nipples, the man's treasure trail, and every cut and perfectly sculpted ab on his chest. A vat of my cream doused his flesh, but he didn't seem to mind at all. In fact, he simply smiled, and said, "I like your white on my black, guy."

"It's a nice mix."

"We're a nice mix," he said, and drew his left palm to the back of my head to begin our next adventure together.

# # # # #

Spent, huffing and puffing for air, I stumbled forward and my face was forced to his hulking black chest. Positioned slightly above me, he instructed, "Lick every drop of your seed up. Don't let it go to waste."

I concurred, directed my lips to his toned chest, extended my tongue, and began to lap up every drop of white Jew-seed from his onyx-colored skin.

"Enjoy it, Adam, every last drop of it."

Honestly, I decided to let him call me by my first name, since I liked it falling out of his plump lips. And between laps, consuming my churn from his nipples, breathing in his sticky male scent, I thought: Chocolate forever. He's now mine, and quite bearable against my skin.

THE CENTER OF ATTENTION
By Eric Summers

Billy played center for as long as he played football, beginning with peewee, then middle school, high school, and now, college. For some reason, coaches automatically put him in that position, bent over with a quarterback's hands up his crotch. Was it his size? He was always the tallest – and widest – kid with the ability to run over anyone headed for the quarterback like a steam roller? Or, was it his round muscular butt, which was so tantalizing in that position. He never thought it was his butt. After all, he had a talent for hiking the ball and immediately knocking down at least three defensive linemen before they knew what hit them. Years of playing football in his hometown of Newport News gave him a reputation, and many a lineman would try to challenge Billy, but by the end of the game, the quarterback on Billy's team would never have a scratch on him.

He entered college with a full scholarship. By eighteen, his frame had filled out quite nicely, and now in his senior year at age twenty-one, he was, as one of the cheerleaders called him, "hunkalicious." Billy was over six-foot-five, weighing more than two-hundred-eighty pounds, with a chest that measured at least fifty-four inches, biceps that approached twenty inches, a waist that although thirty-eight inches was tight and ripped, quads that measured over thirty inches and of course, that big round muscular butt. While many of his teammates were using steroids and other enhancements, Billy had no desire to do anything that wasn't natural. He didn't have to as he was one of the lucky few who could get more muscular just from looking at a dumbbell. To make his teammates more jealous, Billy had inherited the best of both his Russian and Moroccan genes – smooth dark skin, strong facial features, green eyes, thick curly hair and bright white teeth. His hands and feet were huge, and he could palm a football with no problem.

Their first two seasons were highly successful with few losses, so the team was quite surprised when their coach resigned under pressure, and a new coach from a Southern university was brought in. And along with that new coach, arrived a new quarterback. The new quarterback was not unexpected as Jerry Garrison had graduated the prior year and was playing pro-ball now. Billy wasn't envious, for he was not looking forward to a pro football career. He was a straight-A pre-med student, and he was actually looking forward to ending his football days. After all, he had been playing center since he was six years old, and all the practices were getting old.

The team entered the locker room silently the day after the announcement of their new coach and quarterback. As they changed into their practice uniforms, there was grumbling about the new coach's reputation, rumors and gossip that Billy didn't care to hear. The advantage to playing center was that all he had to do was remember when to hike the ball, plow forward and hope he hadn't hurt a defensive lineman – too badly.

After changing, they ran out to the field and lined up, awaiting the introductions.

Billy looked to his right and spotted a tall, black man with an almost equally tall, but younger, black man beside him. The older man looked to be in his mid-thirties, around six-foot-three and muscular. Billy guessed he played football in his youth and maintained his athletic physique. He was wearing a tight white polo shirt that accentuated his large chest and bulging biceps and blue coaching shorts that did little to hide his full basket. He was wearing a cap, but Billy could tell the man had a shaved head, and the hat did not hide the fact that he was perhaps the most handsome man he had ever seen with dark smooth skin and a bright smile surrounded by thick sexy lips. The younger of the two looked to be about Billy's age and maybe only an inch shorter if that much. He was muscular but leaner than the older man. His hair was cut short, and he had high cheek bones, a wide sexy mouth and big dark eyes. He was wearing a green practice jersey and matching sweat pants, but they weren't nearly as tight as the coaches, which is why he probably didn't look as muscular at the moment.

The two men approached.

"I'm Coach Clifford Montgomery, and this young man is your new quarterback, Karl Johnston," the older man said with a bit of a Southern twang Billy recognized, for they were from the same part of Virginia that he was. "Assistant Coach Frase will run you through your drills today ... Which one of you is Greenberg?"

"I am," Billy answered.

"You come with Karl and me," Coach Montgomery said as he signaled for Billy to follow.

As Billy left his teammates, he shrugged his shoulders but did as he was told and caught up with the new coach and quarterback.

"I think it's important that a center and quarterback get to know each other intimately. You two will have to work closer than anyone else on the team, you understand, Greenberg?" the coach asked.

"Yes, sir," Billy responded.

"Good."

Karl just looked back at Billy and smiled.

They continued walking in silence until they reached the locker room then went back to the room that was usually used for rehabilitation with its massage tables, whirlpool and other useful equipment. Billy notice the coach had moved some things around and created a large area in the middle of the room with a section of workout mats. Needless to say, Billy was a little confused. After playing football in the same position for more than fifteen years, he was used to new coaches, but never had he been brought into a situation with just the coach and quarterback.

"I hear you aren't heading for the pros after college? They say you're going to medical school," Coach Montgomery said.

"Yes, sir, I've always wanted to be a doctor. Playing football was a way of getting scholarship money, and what I didn't spend on undergrad, I can use for medical school," Billy answered expecting the coach to give him the same spiel he always got about how with his talents he should go pro and all.

"Good for you," the coach said, surprising Billy. "You'll have a longer career as a doctor and be able to walk without pain after age thirty as well."

"Wow," Billy responded. "You're the first coach to give me that response."

"Johnston here is also pre-med, and the sexy fucker wants to be a surgeon, so I need for you to protect him, so he doesn't injure those hands," Coach Montgomery informed him. "I am not all that keen on playing pro unless you're too stupid to become something else. All that money and a broken body never make for a good combination."

Karl smiled, while Billy wondered if he actually heard the coach call him a sexy-fucker. This wouldn't be too shocking, for coaches and players usually referred to each other with sexual innuendoes and pet names all the time. It was a male-bonding thing, yet there was something about how he said it and the fact that Karl smiled and still had not said a word.

"Damn, a surgeon. Cool. I'm going to become an OBGYN," Billy said directly to Karl.

"All that pussy? Can you handle it?" Karl finally spoke, and what a deep, sexy voice he had, Billy thought as he smiled back at his new quarterback.

"OK, enough of this flirting, love birds, let's get to work," the coach said. He then handed Billy a football. "Greenberg, I want you to practice hiking to Johnston. I don't want any fumbles, none. You hear me?"

They both nodded as Billy bent over to hike the ball. The room was particularly hot, and Billy was dressed in all his pads. He was thankful he had not put on his helmet or he would have passed out.

"Aren't you curious what it's on?" Karl asked.

"Oh yeah," Billy said. "It's just that this is strange for me. I've played center for as long as I can remember, and I never had to practice hiking like this in a room away from everyone."

"You'll find I have new ways of doing everything," Coach Montgomery said. "Before we get started, why don't you get out of those pads; it's hot as fuck in here, and I don't want your parents crying to me when you die of heat exhaustion."

Billy turned to leave the room, when the coach stopped him. "Where the hell are you going?"

"To put on some sweats," Billy said.

"Forget the sweats," the coach said. "Just take off the pads. We're all men here. Hell, you've seen parts of your teammates they've never seen themselves every time you girls shower together."

Billy turned around and took off his practice jersey then his shoulder pads. He was wearing a white T-shirt underneath that was soaked with sweat and clinging to every muscular inch of his torso, but he decided to leave it on. He then took off his shoes and his football pants. Now he was just standing there in a jockstrap that did little to contain his huge basket. His teammates had teased him for years about his big balls and thick swinging dick, so he waited for the usual comments. None came. The coach and new quarterback sort of looked but were all business, and Billy was grateful.

"On thirty-two," Karl said as Billy bent over once again. Karl placed the back of his hand against Billy's balls and formed a cup with the other facing up, waiting for the ball, and began, "Twelve, sixteen, thirty-two ..." and before he could say hike, Billy had launched the ball between his legs, into Karl's hands and was propelling forward before Karl knew what hit him, dropping the ball.

"They said he was the quickest center ever, Johnston," Coach Montgomery said with a chuckle as Karl picked up the ball. "He's already knocked down three guys, and a fourth is gonna grab that ball ... Coach Phillips already warned me about you, Greenberg."

Billy smiled, but he was not the cocky type, so he felt a little sorry for Karl. "Sorry about that. Let's try it again."

"You're gonna take a little getting used to," Karl said as he wiped some sweat off his brow. "This one on three."

He bent over again, and Karl began, "Seven, four, twenty-two, three …" and again he dropped the ball as Billy hiked with lightning speed and lurched forward, but this time the coach was standing right in front of him, so he stopped just short of knocking him over.

"Fuck!" Karl said frustrated.

"Greenberg, bend over," the Coach said. "Watch, Johnston." And the coach took the quarterback's position behind Billy. "You gotta slam the back of your hand up there," and he firmly slammed the back of his right hand against Billy's balls, then formed a cup with the other hand below it waiting for the hike. It wasn't enough to hurt, just enough to send a shiver up Billy's spine. "And hold them there. You should place them in just the right position to lift this big sexy ass off the ground." And with that, he lifted Billy off his feet, leaving the center to use the ball as a support to keep from falling flat on his face. The coach then gently put him back down. "That way, no matter when he hikes the ball, you won't drop it. Now you try."

When the coach removed his hands, Billy actually missed them then he realized his dick was starting to swell a bit, and some pre-cum was leaking out. Now, he wished he had gone to get those sweat pants. He hoped that if he continued to sweat as much as he was now, his jock might be too wet for anyone to notice.

"On twenty-three." Karl resumed his position, this time slamming the back of his hand up Billy's crotch, then forming a cup with the other hand. He then attempted to lift Billy up, but he couldn't, so he just began, "Twelve, twenty, sixteen, twenty-three …" and this time he held onto the ball, but not before almost dropping it again.

"You're getting it … again," the Coach said.

Billy quickly assumed the position before they could notice the pre-cum or the fact that his dick was starting to grow.

He really wished he could get his sweats.

"On seventeen, this time," Karl said. "Wait a minute; it's too fucking hot in here." Then Karl kicked off his shoes, pulled off his sweat pants and removed his shirt, wearing nothing but a jockstrap himself. Billy could see all this when he looked through his legs. Now he knew he was in trouble, for Karl was a brown-skinned god. He then slammed his hand against Billy's balls, but this time he slid them up and down just a tiny bit. "Damn, your butt is all sweaty," Karl complained.

"Just get to it," Coach Montgomery said.

"Thirteen, four, fifty-six, forty-two, forty-three, sixteen, seventeen ..."

Billy hiked and lurched forward, and when he turned around, Karl had the ball firmly in his hand and a big smile on his face. He looked over at the coach who had taken off his shirt, and he really worried about that wet spot on his jock.

"Again," the coach said.

Billy assumed the position for three more hikes. By now, both Billy and Karl were covered in sweat, and Billy had finally removed his wet T-shirt. On the fourth try, Billy waited for the familiar slam of Karl's hand, but it didn't come.

Instead, he felt something soft and realized it was Karl's tongue on his ass!

"Oh man, I just couldn't help myself," Karl said between licks. "I couldn't stare at this beautiful butt a minute longer."

Billy looked up and saw the coach's bare feet in front of him. With his hands still on the ball, he looked further up, and Coach Montgomery was standing there wearing nothing, not even a jock, and his long thick, dark brown cock was pointing straight out above Billy's head. The coach then squatted down, looked the surprised center in the eyes, and said, "You are one beautiful man." Then, he planted his thick full lips on Billy's, and they made out swapping spit and encircling each other's tongues. He never took his hands off the ball, and he no longer worried about the wet spot as his jock was one sticky mess with the coach's tongue in his mouth and Karl's tongue all over his ass.

Karl reached up and grabbed the waist band of Billy's jock to pull it off, or at least he tried for the center's dick was so big and hard, it was making it difficult. Karl reached between Billy's thighs and freed

125

the obstruction, giving the sweat and pre-cum coated dick a nice stroking while he removed the jock with the other hand, never letting his tongue leave that hot ass in front of him.

The coach continued to make out with him, and Billy didn't want him to stop, but the coach left the center's mouth for just a second, and replaced his tongue with his long, thick cock. Billy finally let go of the ball and grabbed the backs of Coach Montgomery's thighs.

No one said a word. There were slurps and moans of satisfaction, but nothing needed to be said.

Billy's ass suddenly felt cool as Karl stopped licking it, slid between the center's thighs and flipped over on his back. He then grabbed Billy's butt and pulled him toward him until the center's enormous cock was aiming at his mouth, and Billy did as directed until he felt the warmth of the quarterback's mouth on his dick. But this position didn't quite work, so Karl slid from between his legs, stood up and guided Billy over to one of the massage tables. He made Billy lie down on his back. The quarterback then bent over and with easy access gave Billy the wettest, most sensual blowjob of his young life, and it was a good thing he had a wide mouth to accommodate Billy's legendary cock. The coach stood near Billy's head and stuck his cock back into the center's mouth.

Karl was stroking his dick and about to blow, when he announced, "Who wants it?"

"I do," the coach said, and with that he bent over just in time for the quarterback to stroke his cock one more time, aiming it at the coach's mouth. Coach Montgomery then took Karl's dick gladly and swallowed every bit of the young quarterback's tasty load.

"My turn. Take it, Greenberg," and the coach blew his huge load into Billy's mouth, which brought him closer to the edge. Billy made sure to get every drop, and the coach did not deny him any.

"Who gets mine?" Billy panted as he let the coach's cock slip from his mouth. Neither the coach nor the quarterback said a word; they just both went down on his throbbing cock, swapping spit between them, and when he shot, one mouth was on it, then the other, and back and forth until he was spent.

126

The coach looked down at Billy and said, "This is how I like for my center and quarterback to get to know each other intimately."

FOOTBALL DADDIES
By Eric Summers

Dan and Bobby had played football together for close to thirty years, from peewee through high school and finally on the same pro team and always on the offensive line. When Dan decided before he turned forty-two that it was time to retire, Bobby came to the same conclusion within minutes. He couldn't imagine playing the game without his best friend around, especially since they had been lovers for the past fifteen years. But, they didn't know what to do in retirement? A lot of football players went into the restaurant business or lent their names to other service industry venues, but Dan and Bobby had no interest in that. Their decision became easier when they heard of a gym that was up for sale in their hometown because the owner had died and his kids had no intention of running it.

They flew down to Elkhart, North Carolina, a small town most maps ignore, and made an offer on the old place. The heirs were more than happy to unload the business and accepted their price without hesitation. Dan and Bobby paid cash and found themselves in the gym business.

Once they found a place to rent until they decided where to live permanently, they began the work of renovating what would become the D&B Fitness Factory. This was one of those old time gyms with benches, free weights, no machines to speak of, and only a couple of stationary bikes serving as cardio equipment. There were mirrors on all the walls and an open shower room that could accommodate eight people at a time.

The work began with getting rid of all the old equipment, so they donated it to an organization that sends fitness gear to developing countries. They ordered all new benches, rubber coated plates, a few basic machines and a couple of treadmills and arc trainers. Their goal was to keep the gym as old-school as possible. They figured if they tried to go fancy, they would not be able to compete with the pretty boy club in the next town.

Elkhart may have been a small town, but football was huge there. Dan and Bobby weren't the only former residents to go pro. Many of their former teammates bought property near the coast, which was only a thirty minute drive from where they were, and once they opened for business, the D&B Fitness Factory filled up every day with quite a few muscle daddies.

Dan and Bobby were all too happy to offer a gym their fellow gray hairs could enjoy. Dan stood over six feet and weighed over two-hundred-fifty pounds of solid muscle with a fifty-inch chest, nineteen-inch arms and maintaining a thirty-six-inch waist, and is fair skin was all covered in salt and pepper fur from his head to his feet. Bobby was smooth and very dark-skinned, but no less impressive with a shaved head to match. He stood barely five-ten, weighed almost two-hundred-twenty-five pounds, but had just as much muscle as Dan with an even broader chest and bigger biceps, but he carried a few inches around his belly. He had one of those tight bellies that many a boy finds sexy. Dan loved Bobby's belly and would come on it every chance he could get. They were both also hung very nicely and circumcised with big round balls, making for a beautiful sight in the bedroom.

The gym was doing very well as they had tapped into a market that the mega-gyms were ignoring. It also helped that they did not require that their members wear shirts, only proper footwear and shorts as long as they cleaned off the equipment after each use. Dan and Bobby did this mostly for their own entertainment since they both enjoyed watching big men get all sweaty and pumped. Even with the lenient rules, the place was kept immaculate, especially the shower room, which was no small feat considering some of the action, rumored to be occurring in there, especially right before the 10:00 pm closing time.

Dan and Bobby had not engaged in any of the antics but had witnessed a few while they were working. They had hired a college senior, who was getting a degree as a physical therapist, to work the evening hours, so they could have a life outside the business, and he was a very hard worker. Miles was also an offensive lineman in high school, who decided not to play college ball for reasons he never explained, so Bobby and Dan took a special liking to him. At twenty-two years old, Miles was already as big as many of the pros, standing at over six-foot-four and over two-hundred-sixty pounds with a solid frame holding a fifty-two-inch chest and twenty-inch arms. He was not only big and muscular, but he was devastatingly handsome as well with cappuccino colored skin, curly black hair and covered in just a touch of curly black fur. When he smiled, men and women melted regardless of their sexual inclinations.

Dan joked that he didn't care how competent he was; Miles had the job the second he applied. What made him even more appealing was his lack of attitude or ego. Miles was a damn hard worker and kept the gym spotless and in order. He never engaged in "activities," nor did he do anything inappropriate. He was quiet and respectful with a pleasant demeanor. He only made one request. Miles wanted to be able to work out after the gym closed for the evening since this would not interfere with his studies. Dan and Bobby suspected Miles was a bit of a loner, for he never received personal calls, was never seen texting nor had any buddies come by the gym to visit. They wanted to invite him over for dinner but somehow never got around to it. What they did learn was that his parents died when he was very young and that he was raised by his grandmother, who recently died. He had no other family and lived in the apartment where he was raised.

Dan and Bobby would usually workout mid-day when the gym was the least busy, but this became a hassle as the business of running a business takes more time than people realize, so they decided to try working out at 4:00 am before they opened. This lasted only a couple of days because getting up at 3:00 am was nearly impossible, too. That was when Dan suggested they follow Miles's lead and workout after hours. This would work since they hired Bobby's nephew to open for them during the week, and they could come in around 7:00 am. Bobby's nephew was competent but not worth the trouble of describing since he spent most of his time at work surfing the net and texting his girlfriend. He was just there to occupy space until Dan and Bobby came in. Miles left the place in such order that there was nothing to do in the mornings, and Bobby told Miles that he knew his nephew was useless, but he needed him for those two hours, so he and Dan could get some rest. Miles never complained. And, Dan and Bobby would keep the place in order while they worked and tended to the business as well, so Miles wouldn't get stuck cleaning up after them.

Around 10:30 pm, Dan and Bobby showed up on the first night they decided to try their new workout schedule. The gym was closed, and the blinds were drawn, but they could see Miles shadow as he worked out inside. They told Miles they would be coming in to work out, so that he wouldn't be startled when the door opened.

Dan and Bobby walked in just as Miles lay down on a bench to perform dumbbell presses with one-hundred-ten-pound weights. They both stopped in their tracks at the sight before them. Wearing nothing but a pair of black 2xist briefs that did little to hide his candy and a pair of New Balance cross trainers, he was pushing the weights up, and his chest was glistening and pumped.

He finished his set and sat up on the bench. "Hey, when you didn't show up at closing, I decided to get comfortable. I'll go get my shorts," Miles said as he greeted them.

"Don't ...," Dan almost shouted.

"... worry about us," Bobby interrupted. "Stay comfortable."

"Are you sure?" Miles asked as he stood up, revealing his body to them for the first time.

"I didn't realize how hot it gets in here with the AC off. Why didn't you reprogram it to stay on for an hour after closing?" Bobby asked.

"I didn't think I had the authority," Miles the ever-dutiful employee responded. "Besides, I prefer it warm when I work out."

Dan and Bobby walked toward the locker room to put away their gym bags, and Miles dropped to the floor to do a set of push-ups. They each glanced at his perfect, big, muscular butt as it went up and down.

In the locker room, Dan took off his shirt as Bobby did the same. "Should we strip down as well?" Dan whispered.

"I might pop wood," Bobby said with a smile. "But, what the hell?!?"

They each stripped down, Dan to a pair of white Calvin Klein briefs, and Bobby to a pair of black trunk briefs of the same brand. They exited the locker room and joined Miles in the gym. Miles went about his chest workout as if everything was normal, and Dan and Bobby worked legs.

Occasionally, they would smile at each other, but Miles was very serious about his workouts, as were Dan and Bobby, and after the initial excitement of being half naked with the college senior wore off, all were grunting and sweating their asses off.

Miles was attempting to do a set of incline dumbbell presses with one-hundred-thirty-pound weights, but was struggling to lift them into position to begin his set. Dan noticed this and offered to help him.

"Thanks, maybe I should begin with the inclines. I can never lift them up this far into my workout," Miles said as Dan walked over. Bobby followed.

"Lie back, and Bobby and I'll hand them to you."

"I'll give you a spot, once you get started," Bobby added.

Miles lay back, and Dan and Bobby on either side of him lifted up the dumbbells and waited until Miles was holding them firmly. Bobby then positioned himself behind Miles to spot him. He managed five reps before he needed assistance, and Bobby helped him with two more.

Once he was done with the set, Miles thanked them, but Bobby remained crouched behind the bench. Dan looked at him, and Bobby motioned downward with his eyes, for he was sporting a hard-on that could not be hidden.

"Let us know when you are ready for another set," Dan said and winked at Bobby.

Miles lay down on the bench again, and was ready in thirty seconds. The kid really did do an intense workout, they noticed.

They helped him get a grip on the dumbbells again, and Bobby hoped Miles didn't see the bulge in his trunk briefs.

Miles did this set and another, and at that point, Bobby's underwear was soaked with pre-cum. He quickly went to the locker room to fetch another pair he hoped he remembered to put in his gym bag. There was a pair, and by the time he had removed the soaked pair and wiped off his dick, he was no longer as hard, but still a little firm. He changed into a matching pair of black trunk briefs, which he was relieved he packed, for he would have to explain the change in wardrobe.

He exited the locker room, and the sight he saw was about to ruin another pair of underwear. Dan was doing a set of squats, and Miles was spotting him from behind. Bobby stood there awestruck at the sight before him, and his dick was now out of control, hard as a rock and leaking like a faucet. When Dan struggled for a few more reps, Miles leaned in closely to help. Two reps later, the set was done.

Miles stepped back, and Dan stepped away from the rack, and he was now sporting a rager equal to Bobby's. He looked over at Bobby, who looked over at Miles, who looked at both of them and smiled.

"I get hard when I work out, too," Miles said. And when they looked down, they noticed his underwear was beginning to stretch quite a bit. He then dropped down and did another set of push-ups, while Dan and Bobby watched.

Dan looked at Bobby and shrugged, and Bobby shrugged back. Miles then finished his set and declared his workout was done, and he was going to take a shower. Meanwhile, the bulge in his briefs was bigger than before, and the head of his dick was sticking out of the waistband. Miles walked past Bobby and into the locker room. Within seconds, the sound of a shower being turned on was heard, and Bobby turned to follow him.

"Are we done working out?" Dan asked as he followed Bobby.

Bobby never answered. He stepped out of his newly pre-cummed briefs and into the shower room where Miles was using the middle-most showerhead. Dan followed suit. Bobby chose the shower to the right of Miles and Dan decided to occupy the one on the left. They watched as Miles soaped himself up and were mesmerized by his pumped, heavily muscled and lathered body and his enormous circumcised cock that stood out and up. Dan and Bobby's big dicks were just as hard.

Dan soaped himself up waiting for Bobby to take the lead if anything were going to happen. And, take the lead, Bobby did. He lathered up his hand, reached down, and began stroking Miles's dick, and he was met with no resistance. Dan then leaned in and kissed Bobby full on the mouth, and their tongues wrestled as Miles reached down and stroked both their cocks. Within seconds, Bobby was ready to pop, so he grabbed Miles's hand to stop the momentum, but Miles proved to be quite strong. That strength was all it took, and Bobby was shouting and shooting a load all over Miles's hand and leg.

Not even a second after that, Dan added to the spunk on Miles and shouted his pleasure as well. The hands of a physical therapist were obviously magic. Dan planted his mouth on Miles's, and Bobby continued to stroke the enormous cock until it shot a load all over the shower wall – a load so impressive that Dan and Bobby almost applauded.

Once he caught his breath, Miles declared, "I've never touched a man before. I have wanted to do that with you guys since the day you hired me."

"You never touched a man?" Bobby asked with surprise.

"Where did you learn to stroke like that?" Dan asked.

"I guess from playing with myself," Miles said as he resumed soaping himself up.

Bobby stopped him, and Dan joined Bobby as they lathered up Miles, taking turns kissing him and stroking him until he shot another load – this time on the shower floor.

# # # # #

Dan and Bobby soon found a 19th Century home that suited them perfectly and settled in nicely. Miles graduated from college and landed a job at a local hospital as a physical therapist.

Does Miles still work at the gym part-time? You bet he does, and he still works out in his underwear after closing every night along with Dan and Bobby. But now, they sometimes shower at the gym or the three of them go home afterward to shower, where they live in a poly-amorous relationship that has "worked out" quite well.

Teammates for life!

A REAL GYM
By Eric Summers

Michael spent more time than he wanted on the road. When he accepted the job as a consultant for the Department of Homeland Security, he thought he would be spending his time in Washington, New York, Los Angeles and Chicago, but that was not the case. Michael found himself waking up in sleepy little towns that cartographers did not take the time to notice. Towns with names like Pungo, Kincaid, Swelterville and Destination, a town so small it was named for being a stop on a long abandoned railroad.

In an effort to ensure that the government would function in the event of a national emergency, Michael's job was to negotiate contracts for bunkers and other sites to house the country's leaders. Uncharted towns made the perfect locations for these future government facilities. The secret was negotiating a deal that did not bring attention to the sleepy hamlets. Many of the civic leaders wanted the attention and hoped to boost their economies with the government contracts. Michael, however, managed to quiet their aspirations with promises of infrastructure improvements, new schools and other necessary projects.

One Monday, Michael arrived in Erlach, Virginia, a town, located southwest of Richmond, but so small, that even the citizens of Virginia's capital had never heard of it. He was pleasantly surprised to find a motel off the main highway through town. At sixty miles per hour, one blink and the motel would have been missed; two blinks and the town would have disappeared.

Michael grabbed his bag from the trunk of his car and knocked on the office door to the Erlach Motel, which was attached to the Erlach Diner, a converted railroad dining car that held the promise of good Southern cooking that Michael always craved. No one answered the door, so Michael walked over to the diner and entered.

It was three-thirty in the afternoon, and only a couple of patrons, mostly elderly gentlemen who looked as if they had retired from a lifetime of dairy farming, were sitting at the counter. Michael sat on a stool and removed his jacket.

At forty-one, Michael looked to be in his prime. He was wearing a dark blue T-shirt and jeans. Michael loved working out, and it showed. He was six-foot-two and weighed two-hundred-forty pounds. Although on the road, Michael managed to find a gym most every place he went, and when none was available, he would work out with the sixty-pound dumbbells and the push-up bars he picked up in a fitness store he stumbled upon in Swelterville. Michael's favorite exercise was push-ups. He would do a set between every exercise even when working out in a gym. If he had a couple of hours free, he would spend them doing set after set of push-ups. Michael lived for the feeling of his chest getting pumped with every rep.

He would often be in a motel room in some hick town, stripped to his briefs, sweaty and pumped from hours of push-ups. Michael would then flex in the mirror and finish his routine by rubbing out a big load from his thick cock.

One of the retired farmers took notice of Michael and stared at him. He was used to being ogled for he was a fine looking man with his olive skin, dark curly hair, thick eyebrows and lashes and dark bedroom eyes. His body was big, hairy and muscular, and Michael was often asked if he took steroids. One look at Michael's large, full balls confirmed that his physique was all natural. Michael liked to eat, and fortunately for him, everything that went into his mouth turned to muscle – everything.

The cook stepped out from the back and walked over to Michael. Michael liked what he saw. The cook was not quite as tall as Michael, but his white T-shirt and stained apron barely contained his powerful black form. There was no hint of hair under his hat, and he had the face of a professional wrestler. Michael noticed the scarred forehead, which was a sure sign of self-inflicted, razor wounds to give a paying crowd the blood they craved. He judged the chef to about fifty or fifty-five, and Michael considered inviting him to his room later that night to see who could do the most push-ups for the longest time. The thought made his cock leak.

"Can I get you anything?" the cook asked.

"Actually, I wanted to get a room for few nights at the motel next door, but no one answered when I knocked," Michael said.

"That's because I'm standing right here," the cook said with a smile. He was missing at least three teeth, probably knocked out by a metal chair in some noisy arena, Michael thought.

"OK, how much is a room?" Michael asked.

"Fifty dollars a night," the cook answered, "paid in advance."

Michael leaned forward and removed his wallet, noticing the cook staring at his flexed triceps. Michael looked at the retired farmer and noticed the man had also never taken his eyes off him. He pulled $150 from his wallet and handed it to the cook while rolling his eyes in the farmer's direction.

The cook looked over at the retired farmer and back at Michael and said, "Don't mind Smitty. Every time a big, good looking guy comes into town, he wonders if he is another of my old buddies."

"From wrestling?" Michael asked.

"Yeah, how did you know?" the cook asked.

Michael motioned to his forehead and said, "You have the battle scars. I follow professional wrestling, but I cannot place you."

The cook put Michael's money in the cash register and reached under the counter, plucking out one of the keys, hooked below. He handed Michael the key and smiled.

"Remember the asshole that always wore an orange mask, wrestled dirty, and was hated by the crowd?" the cook asked.

"You're the Southern Terror?" Michael asked, and he almost shot a load in his briefs.

"The one and only," the cook said. "So, you want anything to eat before you check in?"

Michael was usually hungry, but he only ordered coffee, explaining, "I really want to work out before dinner. There wouldn't happen to be a gym in this town, would there?"

The cook poured him a cup of coffee and said, "Believe it or not there is. It is located in the building behind the motel."

Michael put cream and sugar in his coffee, stirred it and said, "Let me guess. You own that, too."

The cook smiled again and told Michael, "As a guest in my motel, you can work out there for free. I warn you, it's just a gym, no fancy machines or prancing personal trainers, or spandexed pretty boys."

The thought of the cook's gym made Michael's cock leak again, and he said, "That's perfect. I haven't seen a real gym in years. Tell me you don't play loud bar music, and I may buy a house in this town."

"Well, you know that house across the street with a for sale sign in front?" the cook asked.

Michael laughed, wondering just how much of Erlach, Virginia, this hot, retired wrestler owned.

Michael checked into Room 24 and put his bag on the bed. He checked his messages, of which there were three from the DHS, one of which confirmed his meeting with the Mayor of Erlach the following morning at ten.

He opened his bag and pulled out his black sweat pants and an old, gray tank top. Michael was never a slave to health club fashion, so he was sure he would blend in at the cook's gym just fine.

He decided to change his underwear, since the pair he was wearing was stained with pre-cum, not an uncommon occurrence for Michael. He never wore a jock strap, preferring the security of tight, form-fitting briefs. He slipped on his sweat pants and tank top and laced up his black Converse hi-tops. He was looking forward to walking to the building behind the motel and having a real workout. It had warmed up a bit, so Michael figured he would not need a jacket for the short walk to the gym. He also didn't bother to take a lock or gym bag, reasoning he would shower in the motel room before going to the diner for supper.

Michael stepped out of his room and made his way around back. The gym was just fifty or so feet from the motel and looked to be an old converted warehouse. Painted on the door was "S-T's Gym." Michael opened the door, and to his surprise, there were quite a few men working out. There was no foyer, only a small office to the left of the door, and two paces in, Michael found himself in the middle of a large weight room. The place was mainly lit by fluorescent light bulbs, the walls were all mirrored, and any surface that was not covered by mirrors was painted a charcoal gray.

Michael first noticed the lack of music; the only sound that could be heard was the clanking of weights and the grunting of men as they struggled against the iron. He also took in a deep breath, savoring the smell of chalk, sweat and testosterone.

As he looked around, he also noticed that most of the men were working out shirtless. No rules about decorum here. This was a real gym. His cock leaked again.

The door to the office opened, and the cook stepped out and put a hand on Michael's shoulder.

"Just like I told you, nothing fancy, but it's mine," the cook said.

Michael turned to look at him and saw that he had also changed his clothes, wearing a pair of gray sweat pants and no shirt. Even past fifty, the man was powerfully built. His shoulders were like cannonballs, and his pecs were two giant plates of muscle. Michael was jealous of the old guy's enormous traps.

"Hey, this is perfect," Michael said.

"Have a good workout," the cook said as he slapped Michael's large, round, muscular ass. It wasn't a playful slap; it was the slap of an athlete, masculine in its intent.

Michael felt his muscles pumping with blood just from standing in this gym, but he came to work out, and he was going to have a workout reminiscent of the first gym he ever joined. It was similar to this one, and he could have sworn the same shirtless muscle gods were also working out there a long time ago.

The gym was hot and humid inside with the only ventilation coming from the narrow rectangular windows located between the mirrors and the ceiling. Michael decided to forego stretching and work out like a man.

No need to warm up, he thought. If I pull a muscle, I'll just grunt and bear it.

His only worry was that he would come during his first set. Michael was glad he was wearing tight briefs and baggy sweat pants for his dick was already getting hard.

He walked over to the bench where a couple of obvious steroid users were working out together, and before he could ask, they offered to let him work in with them.

Wow, Michael thought. No attitude. Just work in with us.

This place was heaven. The guys were not only big, muscular, hot and half naked, but also they were gentlemen. But of course, they were all gentlemen; they were all between forty and sixty – that perfect generation between attitude and troll.

Michael worked out harder than he had in years, working in a set with this pair of partners and that pair of partners. He benched, he pulled, he curled, he rowed, he squatted, and he lifted. A couple of the guys kidded him about how he did a set of push-ups after each exercise, but when Michael decided to remove his loose tank top before a set of dumbbell flyes, the men took notice, and a couple of them also dropped and did twenty. His hairy chest was so pumped and his big round nipples so hard that Michael could not even see his large feet when he looked down.

As it turned out, most of the guys were old friends of the cook's and retired wrestlers, too, many of them from the days of local circuits before the extreme professional wrestling of today. Although in the ring he was the Southern Terror, the cook was popular in the arena locker rooms, and when he retired to Erlach and opened the diner, the motel, and the gym, many of his former colleagues soon followed, taking up farming or just retiring and enjoying the simple life.

The weight room started to thin out after an hour, but Michael was enjoying the place so much that he decided to keep working out. Before long, the only two guys left in the weight room were Michael and the cook.

"Don't you have to go back to the diner," Michael asked him.

"We don't get busy until about seven, so my two waitresses handle the kitchen and the floor until then," the cook said. "The gym closes at six-thirty, so if you want to get in a shower, you will need to now."

"Oh, I was hoping to work out some more," Michael said.

The cook furrowed his brow and pounded Michael's pumped chest with his fist and said, "If you do another set, you are going to bust an artery. Hit the showers, we open at eleven tomorrow. You can come in then and work out for seven hours if you want."

"That's OK, I was going to shower in my room, thanks," Michael said.

The cook grabbed Michael's shoulder and said, "You will be better off showering here. The showers in the motel will barely hold you, and besides the pressure sucks. It's a dump, but it's my dump, and I wouldn't lie to you."

Michael told the cook he didn't bring a lock or a change of clothes, but the cook would have none of it. He told Michael that these guys could be trusted and just to go commando when he walked back to his room. Michael worried that if he showered with these guys, going commando in his loose sweats would cause him a great deal of embarrassment.

The cook kept his hand on his shoulder and guided him back to the locker room. Michael had no choice.

The locker room was steamier than the weight room, and Michael could hear four or five guys in the shower laughing and talking. He located an empty locker and started to untic his hi-tops. The cook stood next to him and did the same. Michael tried thinking of dead kittens and fat women with hairy vaginas in an effort to keep from getting hard, but it only semi-worked. He hoped that straight guys did not look at another guy's dick, and when he stripped off his sweats and briefs, he took a deep breath. The cook was naked at this point and grabbed two towels, throwing one to Michael.

He looked at Michael's large endowment, including his huge, hairy balls and smiled.

"Damn kid, was your father a buffalo?" the cook said. "Is there anything small on you?"

Michael blushed and wrapped the towel around his waist catching a glimpse of the cook's ample manhood in the process. He was happy the man was circumcised as he was not a fan of foreskin. Michael figured if he was going to look, he might as well enjoy the view.

He walked toward the shower, following the cook. The shower room was as old fashioned as the weight room – just a big, open, tiled room with ten shower heads. Five of the big guys, including two of the men who let Michael work in with them on the bench were showering and talking. To Michael's surprise, one of them was soaping up the other's back, and the one getting lathered was sporting a raging hard-on.

Michael averted his eyes and turned on the shower next to the cook. Showering was the only thing Michael enjoyed more than push-ups, and he stood with his hands on the tiles and let the water cascade from his head down his back. He enjoyed the feeling for quite a while. Lost in the warmth of the spray, Michael closed his eyes and turned around to let the water hit directly on his back. He then reached behind himself and spread his butt cheeks to let the warmth hit every crevice. As he turned his head and opened his eyes to locate a bar of soap, he didn't see one in the dish under his shower head, so he looked across the room. The two guys who were enjoying each other's company were now soaping up with the other three guys. Hands were everywhere. Michael's dick started getting hard, but at this point, he didn't care.

The cook grabbed Michael's arm and placed a bar of soap in his hand.

"Is this what you're looking for?" he asked Michael.

Michael thanked him and started lathering up his hair and then his face. He rinsed the soap from his head, and then he started with his shoulders and worked the lather slowly down his big, pumped, hairy, muscular body. He enjoyed every inch of himself. He slowly soaped his raging nine-by-seven-inch boner and lathered his hairy, buffalo balls. The guys were watching him and from the looks of their own boners were enjoying the show. That didn't stop Michael.

He bent over to soap up his legs, and when he did, he felt a hand on his back. The cook, with his own bar of soap, proceeded to lather up Michael's back, and when Michael stood up, the cook put one hand on Michael's shoulder, and with the other, he lathered Michael's large, round, muscular ass. He was gentle with his touch. The cook squatted down and lathered Michael's legs, slowly with up and down strokes. Michael resumed lathering his chest, stomach, arms, shoulders, and neck. Then, the cook rose and lathered Michael's ass and back again. With his other hand, the cook reached around and put his meaty paw on Michael's aching cock. The huge, mushroom head was swollen, and his balls were ready for release.

Michael continued to lather his chest, shoulders, biceps, triceps, and forearms, and he reached around to lather his own huge lats.

The cook firmly but slowly stroked Michael's hard soapy cock, and after just a few seconds, Michael shuttered and blew a load into the center of the shower room. The sight of Michael coming sent the other five muscle-heads over the edge, and each of them spunked the shower room floor, too. The cook's own large dick creamed Michael's hip, and he continued to stroke Michael's cock until he was sure those big balls were empty.

With everyone's needs fulfilled, the men in the shower finished rinsing themselves off and left the shower room without saying a word, the cook and Michael included.

Michael pulled on his sweats and slipped into his hi-tops, carrying his briefs, tank top and socks back to his room.

He then changed into a fresh pair of white briefs, jeans and an orange T-shirt and walked over to the diner. Michael took a seat at the counter, and the cook came out in the same outfit he was wearing when Michael first met him. Nothing was said of what just took place in the shower room.

Michael understood that it was just men, big muscular men, bonding after a good, healthy workout.

The cook smiled at Michael and recommended the fried chicken, mashed potatoes, green beans and cornbread. Michael didn't argue. He trusted the cook's judgment, and with the first bite, he knew the cook was right.

While he was enjoying a cup of coffee and fresh apple pie, the cook came over to Michael and leaned on the counter in front of him.

"So, what's your business in town," the cook asked.

"I am here to meet with the Mayor about some government business," Michael said.

"At ten tomorrow morning?" the cook asked.

Michael looked at him and asked, "Are you the Mayor, too?"

"And your last name must be Greenberg," the cook said.

They both laughed.

"Good," the cook said, "Tomorrow, after our meeting, you can come back over to the gym, and I will put you through a real workout."

And Michael asked, "How many push-ups can you do?"

Two years later, Michael bought the house across the street, and he would always shower at the gym after his workouts.

THE GUY DOWN THE HALL
By Eric Summers

I really dreaded moving out to a complex in the burbs, but after my upstairs neighbor shot her husband and missed, sending a bullet through her floor and into my apartment, my friends convinced me it was time.

So, here I was in one of those secure buildings with 500 neighbors. That is 500 people who walk by you without smiling, who look at you strangely when you say hello, and who turn up their noses when they see your dog, even though it is a pet-friendly building. I always lived in bad neighborhoods, where people say hello because if you don't know your neighbors, you won't know whether someone is a gang member, mugger or a rapist. It is not that I was too poor to move; I was just too comfortable, paying a low rent and making excuses.

After a few weeks, I made up my mind that no one was going to say hello to the new black guy in the building and that was just how it is with this "station of society" as Hyacinth Bucket would say on *Keeping Up Appearances.* I came back from walking my dog, who was in her twilight years, when the fire alarm went off. I never lived in a building with an alarm, so I scooped up my dog (she had gone deaf and partially blind by then, so in order to evacuate, it was better that I carry her), and we made our way to the stairs. I had moved to the top floor for obvious reasons (bullets tend to go down rather than up). Outside it was raining, and all I was wearing at the time was an undershirt and shorts. After fifteen minutes, we were given the all clear and made our way upstairs. The whole way, no one said a word. They didn't even comment about my dog and why I was carrying her.

Once on our floor, I put Lucille down, and we walked back to my apartment. As we reached my door, my neighbor from around the corner came around and said, "Hey, I see we had another false alarm."

I was surprised for two reasons. One, he said something to me, and two, he was wearing a sleeveless shirt and boxers. What a sight. He was a little over six feet, maybe a drop over two-hundred pounds, with dark hair and eyes and the most fit build I had ever seen, or could see from what was exposed. He was also half my age at around twenty-five.

I had picked up Lucille at that point to keep her from running into him, being partially blind and all, and that made my bicep bulge. I should let you know that I am over six feet myself and close to two-hundred-sixty pounds and a professional trainer and competitive bodybuilder. Approaching fifty, when not in competition, I carry an extra inch or two around the waist, and that is all I will admit.

"False alarm?"

"Yeah, the burger joint downstairs tends to set off alarms all the time. My name's Matt, by the way."

"Nice to meet you," I said as I extended my right hand and shook his. I also put Lucille back down on the floor. "This is Lucille; she's pretty old, deaf and partially blind; that's why I picked her up, so she wouldn't bang into you." And then I shut up, realizing I was giving more information than was necessary and probably because this was the first conversation I had with anyone since I moved in.

"And, your name?" he asked.

"Oh, yeah. I'm Martin."

At that point, he started staring at my arms, and my shirt was still wet from the rain, so his eyes glanced over my pecs as well. "Hey, my fiancé and I are throwing a little party tomorrow night around seven. Come on over. We're in five-eighteen."

"Sounds good," I answered and watched as he turned and went back to his apartment. I also hoped he never wore more than a T-shirt and boxers in the future.

As it turned out, I answered too quickly, since I already had plans the next night with a couple of friends to have dinner. So, the next afternoon, I bought a bottle of wine and knocked on five-eighteen.

Matt answered the door, dressed similarly to the night before.

"Hey, Martin, what's up?"

I handed him the wine and said, "I answered too quickly. I have plans tonight, and I didn't want to blow you guys off and just not show up. Here, this is a thank you for the invitation."

"You didn't have to do that," he said in protest.

"I insist. My mother raised me right," I answered. "Can I ask you a question?"

"Sure."

"Do you own pants?" I asked with a grin.

He laughed, and I heard a woman's voice in the background, "I'm so glad you said that." She appeared from another room, and she was gorgeous and a little thing about half his size. "I'm Gina. Thank you for the wine. I'm sorry you can't make it. He promised to wear pants tonight."

We laughed, and I said my goodbyes.

It was a few weeks before I saw him again. I go to the gym very early and am usually out the door around a quarter to five in the morning. I ran into him one morning as he was headed to his gym, and we exchanged pleasantries, and this became an occasional occurrence. Although beautiful to behold, I made up my mind after meeting his fiancé that he was off limits, and I was never into "flipping" guys anyway. I am too old to go around blowing straight guys, besides I never saw the thrill in that. I never said it out loud, but anyone can figure out I am a big fag from the rainbow star on my front door to the rainbow tattoo on my shoulder to the parade of flaming queens, who are my friends, who would drop by for dinner. Besides a fifty-year-old personal trainer/competitive bodybuilder is a dead giveaway.

One morning as I headed out my door to the gym, I saw a shirtless body walk by and noticed it was Matt. He was wearing very short, gray running shorts that were not unlike the ones President Clinton would wear early in his administration. I yelled at his back, "It is freezing outside. I just came back from walking Lucille."

149

He stopped and turned around, and I saw his bare torso for the first time. He didn't shave and had the perfect amount of dark hair and that theory about him having the most fit body I ever saw was confirmed. I immediately thought that if this guy has a big dick there is no God.

"They say it's seventy outside." He smiled that beautiful smile as I said this.

I walked up to him and got a better look and thanked myself for putting on a tight jock that morning. (I said I was not into flipping straight guys, but that didn't mean he couldn't turn me on.)

We walked over to the elevator and stepped in.

He hit the L and asked if I had an early client.

"No, just working out this morning," I answered.

"Cool, we should work out together sometime," he said.

And then, my odd sense of humor took over when I asked, "Can I pull one of your nipples?"

He looked right at me, smiled and said, "I wish you would."

And, I did. And he leaned in and planted his mouth on mine while simultaneously hitting the red button, stopping the elevator between floors. His tongue was down my throat before I could protest, and I decided not to protest and felt up that perfect body.

I finally came up for air and with a gasp asked, "What about your fiancé?"

"We're both bi," he said and proceeded to remove my shirt and pull down my shorts.

In the time it took for me to fully comprehend what he said, my jock was around my ankles, and my dick was in his mouth. He had pulled his shorts down and was stroking his cock while working mine, and I figured we didn't have a lot of time, and he figured we didn't have a lot of time, and he sucked me for points and knew I would blow any minute, and I tried to get him off my dick, so I could get at his, but he was insistent, and I just shot my load, and he swallowed every drop while jerking his and shooting between my legs and hitting the wall of the elevator. It all happened so fast, that I was still comprehending what happened when he stood up, pulled up his shorts, and I retrieved my shirt, jock and shorts, and he hit the button, and we stepped out of the elevator.

"Have a good run," I said as he took off.

A few weeks later, his fiancé went to visit her parents, and he came over, and we did it again. This time, however, we took our time. He has since married Gina, and their wedding was beautiful. And on occasion, he stops by for a little pre-run work out.

CLOTHING OPTIONAL
By Eric Summers

After a seven-hour drive through rural southwestern Virginia, a few miles across the Tennessee line, and down a very dusty country road, I arrived at the TimberBear Campground. I had read about it online and decided to try a different kind of vacation, but after being buzzed through the gate, if you want to call it a gate, and driving up to the main cabin, if you want to call it a cabin, I was beginning to rethink my idea of an alternative getaway.

Between the geezer who checked me in and the one who pointed out my cabin, there were a total of seven teeth. I drove down the hill to the far side of the grounds past what I assumed was the pool and bath house, a couple of campers and trailers, and spotted little duplex-like cabins lined up in a row. Mine was number 6 – 6B to be exact since it was a duplex of sorts.

It may have been late September, but the weather begged to differ, with temperatures in the nineties and not a cloud in sight. I heard they were suffering through a drought, and by the looks of the layer of dust on my 1977 AMC Matador Coupe, they weren't kidding.

What I didn't see were very many people. I guessed it was late in the season, which was fine, since I am not fond of crowds. I parked around back and unpacked my car. Being this was a clothing optional campground, I didn't have to pack a hundred outfits for a change the way I did for that miserable cruise my best friend talked me into taking.

"Nice ride," came a voice from behind me.

"Thanks."

"1974?"

I turned to face what appeared to be a post-op FTM transsexual wearing only cut-off shorts. "1977 AMC Matador Coupe Barcelona Edition ... it was my grandmother's."

He walked over to my car, and I hastily walked around front to 6B, opened the door and took in the décor. "Early trailer park" would best describe the room, for the cabin was just that, a room. There was a bathroom with a shower stall, and that was about it.

I unpacked what few things I had with me then changed into my swim trunks to take in what little daylight was left in the afternoon. I don't know why I put on my swim trunks since they would be coming off as soon as I arrived at the pool.

I am a former powerlifter and have continued to work out hard since ending my competition days in the late 1980s, which enables me to maintain my thickly muscled physique. I am not what you would call bodybuilder cut, but at five-eleven and over two-hundred-seventy pounds, I am a lot of man, and I have a pretty thick cock and big balls that swing nicely if I do say so myself. I am not self-conscious about my body, but I am aware that there are those with a lot more definition and much prettier faces. The best way to describe my face is that it is that of a bouncer, which is what I do for a living, and my nose has taken its share of punishment as well as my jaw. I get my share of ass when I want it, but I have found that as I grow older and especially after a certain age, I don't crave it as much as I used to. I figure I have done all I care to do in bed, so if I find myself rolling around naked with someone, it better be special.

I chose an empty chaise at the pool, which wasn't difficult since there were about four people there, and took off my trunks, lay down and took in what sun was left for the day.

I was bored already.

After what seemed hours, but was only about thirty minutes, I gathered my things and made my way back to my cabin.

I was kind of tired from the drive and having put in a long shift the night before, so I took a shower in the tiny stall and decided to take a nap.

I never realize how tired I was. When I opened my eyes, it was pitch black in the cabin, and the clock next to the bed indicated it was 2:11 – AM! I hadn't slept like that in years. I was sprawled out naked on top of the bed and sporting an erection that could hammer nails.

154

I got out of bed and looked out the window. There was no one around or lights on, so I opened the door and stepped outside, stark naked and still pretty hard. I stretched my arms and let out a big yawn, when I heard, "Hello." I just about jumped out of my skin.

I had a neighbor in my duplex. Standing at just over six feet, he wasn't a bad looking one either. He was around my age, black, bald, with a mustache, a nice muscular chest – and everything else – and wearing boxer briefs. I immediately hid my cock with my hand.

"Hey, sorry about that ... I didn't think anyone would be out here."

"No problem," he replied then he turned his attention back to his cell phone. "I can't get any bars."

"Isn't it late to be making calls?" I asked while still standing there willing my dick to go down, which it eventually did.

"I've been trying to get a hold of our office overseas all day. Ahh fuck it," he said, then flipped his phone shut. "I guess I should just go to sleep."

"I just woke up from a nine-hour nap," I said with a laugh. "I think I'll see if the pool is open all night."

"The pool is closed, but the steam room and sauna are open all night. They're in the bath house right next to it," he said, obviously having visited there before.

"Thanks, either one sounds good right now."

He went back into his cabin, and I into mine. I brushed my teeth to get rid of the dead rat taste and hoped my breath didn't offend my neighbor. I grabbed two towels – one to sit on in the sauna or steam room and one to dry off with. I didn't bother putting on a pair of shorts and just wrapped a towel around my waist, and slipped on my flip-flops, grabbed a jug of water, then stepped out.

The steam room looked as if a sloppy orgy was played out just hours before, so I chose the sauna. After figuring out how to switch it on, filling the bucket with water to pour over the coals, I hung one towel on a hook outside the door, and slipped off the towel around my

155

waist and laid it on the bench, sat down, leaned back, closed my eyes and relaxed.

I started to sweat almost immediately and took a healthy swig from the jug of water. I then wiped the sweat from my chest down my stomach and along my cock, which started getting hard again. I didn't care, figuring no one was going to come in at this hour, and if they did, whatever.

Wiping sweat across my cock turned into gentle stroking until it was standing right up again ready to do some carpentry work. I closed my eyes and continued gently stroking my dick.

I was starting to feel pretty relaxed and a bit too horny when the door to the sauna opened. I opened my eyes and saw that my cabin mate had entered, and this time he wasn't wearing the boxer briefs.

He walked right over to me without saying a word, leaned down and planted his mouth on mine. We proceeded to make out and wrestle our tongues, while he reached down and grabbed my dick, and I switched my hand from my dick to his, which was also ready to hammer a few nails and had the heft to do so.

The guy was a great kisser, and he apparently thought I was to, which I am of course, but his moans didn't hurt my ego. When his mouth left mine, I missed it immediately, until he hopped up on the bench with his feet on either side of me, his hands on the wall behind me, and his huge cock pointed at my face.

I opened my mouth, let him shove it in, and grabbed his balls. He fucked my throat like a champ, and I didn't gag at all. When I could feel he was getting close, he increased his rhythm, then pulled out and shot a big load all over my face while I held onto his balls.

When he was drained, he hopped down from the bench, got down on his knees and swallowed my cock. It only took a few seconds for him to empty my balls into his hungry mouth. He then stood up, leaned in and licked my face clean before planting his mouth on mine again as we tasted our comingled loads in his mouth.

He then winked, turned around and left. I never saw him again.

STEPBROTHERS
By Eric Summers

With spring semester over, Adam headed home for the summer before his senior year at State University. His mother had remarried in the last month, and she and her new husband were still on their honeymoon, so Adam knew he was coming home to an empty house.

After a three-hour drive, he was happy to be pulling up in front of the house, and he noticed the hatchback parked in the driveway and figured it must belong to one of his new stepfather's kids, probably checking on the house.

Adam pulled his suitcases out of the trunk and walked up the walkway, let himself in, and walked right up the stairs. After a long drive, he was in no mood to talk to anyone.

He put the suitcases in his room, and the first thing he noticed was how hot it was in the house. If one of his new step siblings was there, why didn't he turn on the AC? Adam shook his head and took off his shirt.

Adam had been lifting weights since he was sixteen. His body was perfectly proportioned and nicely muscled at five-foot-eleven and one-hundred-eighty-five pounds. He inherited his mother's smooth chocolate brown skin and his father's large round ass, among other large assets.

He walked downstairs to turn on the air conditioning. While adjusting the thermostat, he heard the front door open and someone saying goodbye, followed by a car speeding away. He remembered his stepbrother from the wedding. Louis was a little taller than Adam at six-foot-one, but he was leaner. His nineteen-year-old stepbrother had straight brown hair and fair features much like his father's, with blue eyes and nice pink lips that begged to be kissed.

Adam remembered talking to him at the wedding and wondering if it would be incestuous to lay his new stepbrother.

"Hey, Adam," Louis said as he extended his hand. The two of them shook hands.

"Dude, what's with not turning on the AC? It's like a fucking oven in here," Adam said.

Louis shook his head and headed upstairs. That was when Adam remembered that Louis was not much of a talker, and from what he gathered from his mother and Louis's siblings, he was not always playing with a full deck either.

Nutty or not, Adam still wondered if the boy liked to play.

He headed back to his bedroom and unpacked his bags. After putting away the last of his clothes and putting the suitcases in the closet, he headed back downstairs to the kitchen for some water. His mother always kept a large jug of water in the refrigerator, and he decided to forgo a glass and drink it straight from the jug. As he was guzzling the water, Louis walked into the kitchen.

"Adam, the man," he said.

Adam quit guzzling for a second and looked at Louis who had stripped to his boxers. The boy was long and lean, built like a swimmer with broad shoulders and a six pack. This pissed Adam off because he knew Louis never worked out, but he did hold out hope that Louis would end up fat when he hit thirty!

"So, Louis, are you living here now, or are you house sitting?" Adam asked him.

"Wouldn't you like to know, bro," Louis said, and he grabbed a soda and headed back to his room.

Adam rolled his eyes and finished the jug. He filled it with tap water, put it back in the fridge and hoped it was full of bacteria for Louis to enjoy.

Adam headed upstairs, walked into the bathroom, stripped and stepped into the shower. While he was soaping up, he thought of Louis, the weirdo, standing in the kitchen wearing nothing but his boxers, and his dick started to grow. Adam had not come in a few days, so he took hold of his favorite toy and rubbed out a big load, barely taking a couple of minutes to do the deed, and hardly making a sound in the process as he learned to stay quiet while jerking off in the dorm.

He finished his shower and pulled the curtain back, grabbing a towel at the same time. Adam was startled to find Louis there flossing his teeth. The house had two full baths, why was he in this one?

Adam tried his best to conceal his cock, which was still half hard. It was difficult enough to hide when it was soft. However, Louis paid no attention to him, so Adam thought he would take one more stab at conversation.

"So, Louis, are you working or going to school?"

Louis stopped flossing and turned around to look at Adam, who had since wrapped the towel around his waist. Then he faced the mirror again.

"No," Louis said. He finished flossing and went into the guest room, shutting the door behind him.

"What a doofus," Adam said to himself. "I hope the little asshole isn't here all summer."

Adam brushed his teeth then crawled into bed.

At three in the morning, Adam was startled awake by some strange sounds. He thought there were cats fucking outside his window, but he soon realized the sounds were coming from the next room. He heard squeaking, then high pitched moaning, more squeaking, and then Louis's voice saying over and over again, "Good boy, good boy, good boy."

Adam never heard anyone come in. Who the hell was Louis talking to? Then he heard him yell, "AHHH AHHH AHHH," so loudly it shook the walls. Adam buried his head in his pillow to keep from laughing. Once the screaming stopped, he then heard Louis saying, "I am such a good boy, oh yeah, good boy, good boy." Then, there was silence.

Adam was still laughing as he thought about his strange stepbrother masturbating and congratulating himself. Then he got hard again, himself, but he was too tired to jerk off, so he rolled over and went back to sleep.

Adam woke up early the next morning and decided to make himself a pot of coffee and work out in the basement gym, provided it was still there. After locating his extra large mug, he filled it with the freshly brewed coffee and headed to the basement.

Since it was still pretty early, Adam decided to work out in just a black cotton jock strap, crew socks and cross trainers. The jock hugged his round butt and displayed his big basket perfectly, and he wished there were someone there to enjoy the view.

Once in the basement, he was happy to see that for the most part his equipment was still where he left it.

He loaded a couple of plates on the bar and secured them with collars. He decided to stretch a bit, and when he bent down to touch his toes he looked through his legs and saw Louis, stark naked and standing right behind him. Adam immediately stood up and turned around.

Louis was standing there with his dick hanging limp but low accompanied by two big, equally low hanging balls, and he was holding a cup of coffee.

"Adam, the man," Louis said. "I took some of your aromatic java." He then turned around and headed back upstairs.

Adam was only pissed because he would now have to brew more coffee.

He slid under the bar and pressed the weights for twelve reps, and he sat up after the set and admired himself in the mirror he had mounted across from the bench. Adam ran his hands over his chest and down his six pack abs. He then flexed both biceps, displaying the high peaks that always earned him attention in the gym at school.

He lay back down and did another twelve reps. With each set, he looked in the mirror and flexed his pecs, bouncing them before doing another double bicep pose.

Adam stood up and removed some of the plates and curled the barbell for ten reps very slowly, keeping his eyes on the vein that ran up his arm. Watching his biceps pump full of blood always turned him on, and his jock was beginning to get tighter.

He put the bar down, and flexed again, doing a crab pose, flaring out his lats and finishing off with another double bicep pose. Adam then did another set of curls.

During his third set, he heard Louis coming down the steps. Adam finished the set and put the bar back. This time Louis was sitting in front of the mirror drinking another cup of coffee, blocking Adam's view of himself. Fucking asshole, he thought, Drinks my coffee and interrupts my workout. However, Adam didn't confront him because Louis was still naked.

"Can I help you, Louis?" he asked.

Silence.

Louis just stared at Adam, studying every inch of him. Adam noticed how Louis was looking at him and didn't know what to make of it.

"Louis, you're sitting in front of the mirror, and I can't watch myself when I work out."

Louis turned and looked at the mirror as if he didn't know it was there. He stood up and leaned on an old dresser that was placed in the basement a decade before.

"Louis, are you just going to stand there?" Adam asked him.

Again, silence.

Adam did another set of curls, watching himself in the mirror when he noticed Louis standing behind him. Louis reached around and felt Adam's biceps with each curl of the bar, running his hands over the pumped muscles. Adam continued his set, enjoying the feel of his stepbrother's hands on his muscles, and he started to get hard again.

Adam curled until he was exhausted, then he put the bar back on the rack. As he looked at himself in the mirror, Louis continued to explore his body with his hands.

Louis felt his stepbrother's lats, tracing his fingers up Adam's muscular back, then he squeezed Adam's softball sized shoulders, and as one hand made its way up Adam's neck the other reached around to feel Adam's pumped chest.

As Louis continued exploring his body, Adam's breathing became heavier. He let his stepbrother enjoy every sweaty, pumped inch of him, and finally, Louis's hand was inside the black cotton jock strap and going for the prize.

As he released his stepbrother's enormous boner, Louis stepped around and brushed his lips against Adam's. Adam opened his mouth and reached around Louis's head drawing him in and kissing him deep, tasting the coffee the asshole had taken without permission. With his free hand, Adam reached down and grabbed the weirdo's hard dick and was impressed with its length and girth. Adam slid his hand up to the swollen head and slicked it with the pre-cum Louis's big dick generously provided.

Louis had managed to get Adam's jock down around his ankles, and they continued to make out while stroking each other's dicks. Louis's free hand continued to explore Adam's pumped body and found a nipple, giving it a hard pull. Adam moaned, but he did not let go of Louis's mouth. Those soft lips were too good to let loose even for a second.

He let go of Louis's head and flexed his right bicep while his stepbrother felt it with his left hand, as they continued to kiss. Louis obviously liked the feel of flexed muscles because his dick would swell and pulse, emitting more pre-cum whenever Adam flexed. This in turn made Adam's thick cock swell up, and he didn't know how much longer he could last.

Their breathing increased, and the stepbrothers were getting closer, but they never unlocked their lips.

Finally, Louis pulled away from Adam's lips and screamed, "AHHH AHHH AHHH," so loud it startled Adam. Then he shot his load covering Adam's belly and chest with pints of cum. The site of his stepbrother's load on his pumped chest made Adam shoot all over Louis, who groaned while Adam was shooting, "You are such a good boy, oh yeah, good boy, good boy." Then, there was silence.

They pulled away from each other, and Adam grabbed a towel to wipe himself off, but Louis stopped him. He bent down and licked his stepbrother's body clean. After he finished his breakfast of cum, he winked at Adam, turned and walked back upstairs without saying a word.

Adam stood there with his half-hard cock hanging out and his black cotton jock at his ankles and watched Louis's round butt bounce as he walked upstairs.

"What a fucking nut job," Adam thought. Then he smiled and hoped all his workouts would end like this one.

LASSO AND TLEM
By Eric Summers

The day was getting late, but according to the old man at the ranch, the next real town in the Arizona Territory was only a dozen or so miles away. He hoped to find a blacksmith when he arrived as Montgomery, his horse, needed new shoes.

The sun was blazing, more than Lasso ever experienced being raised in Virginia. Sure, the summers were hot, but nothing like this. Lasso didn't know much about temperatures, but he guessed this to be hot enough to cook beans without a fire. He stopped at a pond, one of just a few he had encountered over the last few days, and he hopped off Montgomery, so the poor horse could get a drink and some rest.

Lasso stretched and decided he better fill his canteen and get a drink himself. He leaned over to the pond and filled his canteen then scooped a few swallows of water into his palm to quench his parched throat. He checked out his reflection in the water.

Saying that Lasso was narcissistic would be an understatement. He was damn good-looking, and he knew it, and if you didn't think he was good-looking, just ask him. He was six-foot-six and thick with muscle. His black, wavy hair was shaggy but fell perfectly over his square face with his dark eye brows, deep black eyes, strong jaw and rare for anyone at that time, perfectly straight teeth framed by full lips.

Lasso reached up and patted Montgomery, the only thing he loved more than himself, and his horse neighed appreciatively.

"I'll walk you the rest of the way, old girl."

Lasso stood up, placed his canteen back in the bag hanging behind his saddle, and grabbed Montgomery's reins.

He walked a few miles before stopping to strip off his shirt, revealing his hairy muscular physique, built from years of ranch work and roping cattle.

165

After about an hour, Lasso spotted what looked to be the beginnings of a town, if one could call it that – just a strip of buildings on a dirt road, maybe ten if that many. He stopped and put his shirt back on before going any further as he didn't want to draw too much attention to himself being so good-looking and all.

As he approached the outskirts of this town, he saw a sign that said, "Welcome to Nemtoh, Arizona, Population 69."

"I guess this is it, Montgomery. Now let's see about getting you some new shoes."

Montgomery answered with an affirmative neigh.

As he walked down the main street – the only street – in Nemtoh, Lasso noticed only a few people, all men actually, walking around. And, all of them, though handsome, every one of them, looked at him with suspicion. He spotted a young blond guy, tall, strapping and looking especially clean for someone in a town like this.

"Excuse me, mister," Lasso called out.

"Yes," the blond answered as he pushed up his hat.

"Is there a blacksmith in this town?"

"What's your name?" the blond asked.

"Name's Lasso, is there a blacksmith?"

"What brings you to Nemtoh?" the blond asked without answering the initial question, and this was beginning to piss Lasso off.

"Look, I'm not here to start trouble. I'm on my way to work at a ranch fifty miles west of here, and my horse needs new shoes."

"What ranch?" the blond asked insistently.

"Jeez, man, what's your problem? Is this some kind of private community? Fuck it! I'll just let my horse suffer until I find the next town." And, Lasso turned his horse around and started to walk back to the main trail.

166

"Wait a minute, Lasso," the blond called out. "It's just that we're a quiet town, and we like to know who's coming through."

Lasso stopped and turned around. He hesitated before speaking, "So, what are you? The goddamn marshal or something?"

"Actually, I'm the mayor, Mayor Bottumzup."

Lasso smiled and stifled a giggle, "Did you say bottom's up?"

"Bottumzup, and I've heard them all. I don't want to see your horse suffer ... the blacksmith is over there," Bottumzup said, pointing to a building across the street. "His name is Tlem."

"Tlem? Thanks," Lasso said as he walked Montgomery over to where the mayor pointed.

"If you need to stay the night, we have a hotel over there," the mayor said pointing to another building with a sign out front that read, "Hothole Hotel – No Women Allowed."

"Thanks," Lasso answered as he continued toward the blacksmith's building then stopped to read the hotel sign again to be sure he saw what he thought he saw. He did. He pushed his cowboy hat up and shook his head, wondering what kind of town he had stumbled upon.

Lasso entered the blacksmith's building slowly and looked around before spotting a very tall, muscular black man, wearing no shirt, a leather apron and those new-fangled dungarees or blue jeans as they called them in California.

"Are you Tlem?" Lasso called out.

The man turned around, and Lasso got a good look at his face, which was very handsome, with a strong jaw and equally full lips like Lasso's, but the blacksmith's muscular torso was devoid of hair, although glistening with sweat, and Lasso felt a stream of pre-cum drip out of his cock and down his left leg.

"Name's Lasso," he said as he reached out to shake the man's hand, "Montgomery here needs a new set of shoes. How long will that take?"

167

The blacksmith shook Lasso's hand and spoke for the first time, "Kinda backed up, I can have her ready by tomorrow morning."

Lasso pulled out his watch. It was getting pretty late, and he wasn't about to make it to his new job before tomorrow anyway. "Sounds good. I guess I'll stay at that hotel tonight. Should I pay you now or tomorrow?"

"I like to be paid when I'm done," Tlem said then he took Montgomery's reigns and led her to a stall where he had water and hay ready for her to enjoy. "See you in the morning, Lasso."

Lasso took one more long look at the blacksmith before heading over to the Hothole Hotel to make sure the sight was etched into his memory.

For a very small town, the Hothole was quite a fancy hotel. But, Lasso figured that they were the only place to stay in these parts as the railroad hadn't even made it this far. The manager was another handsome Nemtoh citizen, albeit a bit older than the others he saw outside. There were a few patrons at the bar, all looking a little too clean for life in the Arizona Territory, but Lasso didn't mind as he had seen enough filthy men since heading west a few months ago.

"How many nights will you be staying, Mr. Lasso?"

"Just the one. Gotta head out to a job on a ranch tomorrow," Lasso answered.

"Very good, sir. That will be three dollars."

Lasso handed three silver dollars to the manager thinking the price a bit steep, but didn't complain.

"Would you be needing a bath? We can launder your clothes also."

Lasso was puzzled, bath, laundry, who heard of such a thing out here? He pretty much gave up on bathtubs since leaving Virginia using ponds and streams to wash up and launder his clothes. "Yeah, that would be good. Pretty clean town you have here."

"Well, Mr. Lasso, just because this is a small town in the Arizona Territory doesn't mean we have to live like Barbarians," the manager said with a wink.

The manager handed Lasso his room key and told him someone would be up to take him to the washroom within the hour.

Lasso didn't realize how tired he was. No sooner had he entered the room, stripped off all his clothes and climbed onto the bed that he closed his eyes and fell asleep.

He was awakened by the sound of someone in his room. As he opened his eyes, he saw what looked to be a young man, who seemed to be a hotel employee.

"I didn't mean to wake you, sir. I was just returning your laundry."

"How long was I asleep?"

"About three hours, sir. You may take your bath now. The washroom is down the hall on the right, and I have filled your tub with hot water. Here is a towel for you," and the young man handed him the softest towel he ever felt.

Lasso climbed out of the bed and wrapped the towel around him, noticing the young man stealing a peek. He exited the room and walked down the hall and located a room marked Wash Room. He opened the door, and there were two tubs in the room, which was decorated as nicely as the lobby, with a wood stove for heating water and nice curtains over the windows. One tub was occupied, so Lasso closed the door behind him and walked toward the empty tub. As he looked over at the other tub, he saw that Tlem was relaxing in the sudsy water.

Tlem opened his eyes and saw Lasso standing there wearing nothing but a towel.

"You finished with Montgomery already?" Lasso asked.

"Yep, that'll be three dollars."

169

"No pockets here, I'll pay you after my bath," Lasso told him as he looked over the blacksmith's upper torso and felt his cock start to swell.

"So why do they call you Lasso?" Tlem asked, looking at Lasso as if he were a meal for the tasting.

Lasso removed his towel revealing his slightly swelling uncut cock, whose foreskin barely concealed the large head, which was already reaching nine inches and still had at least two to go. "That's why."

Tlem licked his lips and said, "Impressive."

Lasso climbed into the tub hoping the water would calm him down. "Why do they call you Tlem?"

Tlem looked over at Lasso, then he stood up and revealed a hefty cock that matched Lasso's in length and girth, but was getting harder by the second. Lasso looked at the muscular blacksmith with his large, hard black cock pointing at him and tried to act nonchalant, although he had been hungry for a big piece of meat for days.

"Beautiful, but what does Tlem have to do with that?"

"Three-legged man was my nickname on the plantation. When they granted me my freedom, I chose the name Tlem."

The blacksmith then walked over to Lasso's tub and leaned down next to him, looking him right in the eyes. Without saying another word, he placed his calloused hand behind Lasso's head and pulled him in for a long hard kiss, and Lasso thought he would shoot his load right there as his big dick reached its full eleven inches in seconds.

With his other hand, Tlem reached into the tub and grabbed the hard member and started to stroke it without losing his mouth's grip on Lasso's. The ranch-hand reached under Tlem and grabbed his hard eleven inches and matched him stroke for stroke. They kept this up for quite a while without releasing their mouths, moaning and breathing hard, and slurping …

"I'm gonna blow, if you keep that up," Tlem said, finally releasing Lasso's mouth.

"Me, too," Lasso answered.

With that, Tlem stood up walked around, so he was behind Lasso's head and leaned down so his cock aimed at the ranch-hand's mouth and continued leaning over until Lasso's cock was aiming for his. Both men needed no instruction as they each began to feast on the other's enormous meat, and it was not long before they both fed each other huge loads of ranch-hand and blacksmith cum.

Finally, releasing Lasso's cock, Tlem said, "For that, I'll give you a discount on the shoes."

"That was all I had to do for a discount?" Lasso asked smiling and looking up at this beautiful blacksmith.

"I'll let you have them for free if you do me one other favor."

"What's that?" Lasso asked.

"My horse, York, needs some release, too, and he kinda took a liking to Montgomery. Let him have his fun ..."

"Wait, I can't have a pregnant horse while working on the ranch ..." Lasso protested.

"Let me finish," Tlem interrupted. "I own a ranch just outside of town. You come work for me, and I'll pay you whatever you were supposed to get where you're going."

"Why should I do that?" Lasso asked.

"Because nowhere else in the Arizona territory are you gonna find a town full of men who like doing what we just did, and you can live in my house and do it with me all the time," Tlem said with a wink.

Lasso didn't need any more persuasion and agreed to Tlem's terms, and both he and Montgomery ended up happy in their new home ...

... and if this were a movie, the next scene would have them riding off into the sunset – naked.

THE ONE GIVING THE ORDERS
By Eric Summers

Another scorcher on Paris Island, South Carolina, and Master Sergeant Masters was ready to call it a day. Seven weeks into boot camp with the latest flock of recruits was taking its toll on Masters, and he swore after week eleven, once they were done with him and off to infantry training, he would retire. Twenty-five years he had spent in the Marines, and he was damn proud of his service to his country. Although he never saw combat, he had trained by last count more than 11,000 recruits – the majority of whom arrived as long-haired pussies and left as jar-headed fighting machines.

His once deep resonating voice had matured to a prematurely raspy quality due to years of yelling orders and berating the greens.

After marching his boys into the barracks, he handed over control to Master Sergeant Earl, completed some paperwork, hopped into his Dodge pick-up, and drove to his home in Beaufort. He had chosen to live off base a few years before when he spotted the little house while out for some R&R one weekend. There was a for sale sign on it, and once he had contacted the real estate agent and taken a tour, he knew it was the home he always wanted. Having always lived modestly, driving an almost thirty-year-old truck at the time and always living on base, he was able to pay cash for the house with a little to spare to fix it up. His favorite feature was the basement. Basements were rare in these parts being so close to the coast, but this house was more than one-hundred years old.

Masters pulled up to the house, parked his truck around back, and hopped out. He inspected his garden then he stretched his arms and let out a roar. Barking orders all day had taken its toll, and at forty-six, he was getting seriously tired of always being in charge. Masters looked down at the garden and noticed some weeds popping up, so he started pulling them out. The sun was baking, so he pulled off his olive-green T-shirt, revealing his dark, muscular torso. All he had on were his fatigues and boots. At six-feet even and close to two-hundred-sixty pounds, Masters was a solid mountain of muscle. Prominent veins popped from his forearms up across his biceps right over his deltoids. His chest was two solid mounds of pectoral muscle featuring protruding nipples – nipples one just wanted to suck and chew on for hours. And, Masters wouldn't have minded that as they were hot-wired right to his gigantic dick.

He continued pulling the weeds and was working his way across the garden, when he heard a vehicle pull up in front of his house. He then heard a door open and shut, then another.

"What have we here?" came a voice at the foot of the garden.

Masters looked up and saw two men, both wearing fatigues and boots and no shirts standing there in his backyard looking at him. He recognized both of them. The man who had spoken was Private First Class Boneman, who finished boot camp a little over a year ago. Boneman was around five-foot-ten and one-hundred-seventy pounds with light blond hair covering his young, muscular body, a handsome face with blue eyes and a blond high-and-tight haircut. Standing next to him was his boot camp buddy, Private First Class Firestone, who was considerably shorter than Boneman, but weighed the same, displaying a thickly muscled frame. The little man had dark features, smooth skin and hauntingly black eyes. One could tell immediately he was not the brightest guy, but sexy nonetheless.

"I think it's our favorite drill instructor, Master Sergeant Masters," Firestone answered.

Masters stared at the two boys, expressionless. He didn't know why they were here, nor did he care. Once the boys were done with boot camp, he was done with them.

"So, growing pretty flowers, Sarge?" Boneman asked as he walked toward Masters with Firestone beside him.

"What do you boys want?" Masters said as he stood up.

Instantly, Boneman lunged toward him while Firestone grabbed his arms and pinned them behind his back. Boneman held a hand at Masters' throat while he grabbed the top of his fatigues with the other hand.

"We're here to have a little fun with our favorite drill instructor," Boneman said as he spit in the sergeant's face.

Masters just stared him down.

Firestone removed his military-issue belt and tied Masters' wrists behind his back, and Boneman grabbed the older man's dog tags and led him into the house. They entered through the back door into the kitchen, where Boneman opened the first door he saw, which turned out to be a broom closet. He opened a second door, which opened to a staircase leading to the basement. After feeling inside the wall for a light switch and turning it on, he continued to lead Masters by the dog tags while Firestone held onto his bound wrists and pushed him from behind as they descended the stairs into the dimly lit basement.

"Woo hoo, lookey here," Boneman said as he scanned the room.

There was a sling hanging down in the middle of the room, off to one side was a wall with permanently attached restraints, a weight bench was situated in one corner, and in the opposite corner was a claw-type bathtub. Interestingly, hanging over the bath tub were chains with wrist restraints attached at the ends. Various brushes, hoses and other odds and ends were sitting on a table next to the tub.

"Get him into the tub!" Boneman barked at Firestone, who did as he was told. Masters tried to resist, but the little muscleman was still able to steer him over and into the tub. Boneman reached up and pulled down the two chains, removed the belt that Firestone had used, while the little man held onto the sergeant's wrists. Boneman grabbed one of his wrists, brought it in front of him, and restrained it on the chain then he did the same with the other. He then pulled the chains up, so Masters' hands were above his head.

Boneman looked him in the eyes, and when he did, Masters spit in his face. Boneman wiped the spit from his face then punched Masters in the gut, which to the young man's surprise was like a brick wall. The feel of the older man's rock-hard abs against his fist sent a shockwave to Boneman's crotch, and he punched him again. Three more punches, and his dick was drooling. Masters only grunted with each punch, being no stranger to pain – and unbeknownst to Boneman, turned on by being gut punched.

"Get his boots and pants off!" Boneman ordered the little man.

Firestone did as he was told, and when Masters tried to resist, Boneman punched him again.

Masters was now standing in the tub only wearing his olive green boxers, which Boneman wasted no time ripping off him.

"Hey Firestone, look at that?" Boneman said as he scanned the big naked man in front of him. "What do you think, eight, nine, maybe even ten?" he continued while pointing to the older man's dick, which was flaccid but hanging a good seven thick inches nonetheless.

"Those hairy balls are as big as apples," Firestone chimed in. "Pretty impressive for a girl with a flower garden."

Boneman chuckled at the little muscleman's joke then he ran his hand down Masters' body then grabbing his nuts, which barely fit in his hand. Masters' dick started to grow with Boneman's handling of his sack.

"Clean him out," Boneman said to Firestone, while still holding the sergeant by the short hairs.

"With what?" Firestone asked dumbly.

Boneman reluctantly let go of the balls and grabbed the hose that was attached to the faucet. It was a chrome hose with a narrow spray attachment at the end, shaped too much like an enema.

"With this … I'll loosen the chains, so he can be on all fours in the tub," Boneman said as he handed the hose to Firestone.

Boneman loosened the chains and guided Masters down, so he was now on all fours with his big, muscular ass in the air. The sight of the sergeant's hole up in the air was almost enough to make Boneman cream his fatigues, and one look at Firestone's pants confirmed that he also appreciated the view.

Boneman turned the tap on lukewarm, and Firestone inserted the hose into the sergeant's hole, and the drill instructor didn't even flinch, for he didn't want them to have the pleasure of knowing how much they were humiliating him.

"Fill him up. I want him clean before I go in there," Boneman said with a smile.

"The hell you will!" Masters protested, speaking for the first time since entering the basement.

Boneman leaned down, cupped Masters' chin and said, "Did I ask you to speak? You aren't in charge here. I am. Maybe it's time you learned to take orders rather than give them. You got that, you miserable motherfucker?"

"Yes, Sir," the sergeant mumbled.

"I didn't hear you, pussy!" Boneman barked.

"Sir, Yes, Sir!" Masters bellowed as his bowels were filled with the warm water.

Firestone removed the hose, and Boneman told him to push. As the water sprayed from his aching hole, it was not as clear as Boneman would have preferred.

"Do it again, and keep doing it until it's clean enough to drink," Boneman told Firestone.

And, again, Firestone inserted the hose. After five times with the hose and evacuating on command, the water was crystal clear, and Firestone used the hose to spray the excess water down the drain.

"Now, we'll get him all cleaned up … the same way he used to order us to clean up that stinky recruit with a scrub brush … what was his name?" Boneman asked.

Firestone answered, "Robert Taylor."

"Yeah."

Boneman removed the enema attachment from the hose and attached a garden sprayer, while Firestone removed his own boots, pants and boxers, then put his boots back on, revealing his own hefty meat, which was secured with a leather cock ring, making his full balls swell.

"I don't want to get wet … man I got to take a piss," Fireman said, while handling his prick.

"Take a piss then; just be sure you aim for his face," Boneman said as he removed his own clothes.

Firestone then positioned himself in front of the sergeant and released a healthy stream of his urine all over Masters' face and hair, while the sergeant just closed his eyes. Boneman noticed how the older man opened his mouth slightly to taste the nasty stream and chuckled at what a pig the man was. Boneman then put his boots back on, and marveled that Firestone was still pissing, when he decided to join in and released a healthy stream from his own thick meat, which was supported with a chrome cock ring, all over Masters' face and head. When they were done emptying their bladders and shook the last drops on the older man, Boneman turned on the hose and sprayed down the drill instructor starting with his head and working his way back to his well worked over hole. He then handed the hose to Firestone, while he pulled the chains bringing the man to a standing position again.

When the two young men looked down, they saw that the sergeant's dick was standing at half-mast and a good ten inches in front of him.

"I knew it would get huge," Boneman said to Firestone, who whistled. "Now scrub him down."

Firestone sprayed the water into a bucket that was next to the tub, filled it with the liquid soap that was on the table, grabbed the scrub brush, and dipped it into the sudsy water. He then started with Masters' head, which was a reach for the shorter of the two men, and worked his way down Masters' entire body until he was covered in suds and clean enough for inspection. Boneman then rinsed the suds off with quite a hard setting on the sprayer, yet Masters refused to acknowledge even the slightest pain or humiliation.

"He's a tough old fart," Boneman said as he turned off the faucet.

"A hot one, too," Firestone said. But, Boneman gave him an angry look for saying anything positive about the older man.

"Let's get him over to the sling," Boneman ordered as he undid the restraints on Masters' wrists. "And if you try anything, you'll be sorry, old man," he said as he looked Masters in the eye, and again Masters spit in his face. Boneman immediately followed with another punch to his stomach. He then punched him two more times, and his own dick reacted at the feeling of the sergeant's rock-hard abs against his fist.

With the position of authority firmly established, they marched Masters over to the sling, lifted him into it, and secured his wrists and ankles, so he was on his back with his powerful legs spread. Surprisingly, the drill instructor's cock got even harder once he was restrained, and almost reached its full eleven by seven inches, when Boneman clamped two clothespins on Masters' large hot-wired nipples. Boneman grabbed the huge dick, gave it a good squeeze, and said, "Too bad you're such a bottom pussy, motherfucker."

Firestone's thick seven-inch cock was standing straight up at this point as he awaited his next order, and Boneman's eight inches were almost at full staff, too.

"Bring me that tin container over there," Boneman ordered as he pointed to the table of supplies. "And that black rubber glove, too."

Masters' eyes popped open.

Boneman looked right at him, and said, "I want to see if my fist'll fit up this big hole of yours. Think you can take it, old man?"

Masters didn't answer, but gave him a look that practically said, "I'll kill you when this is all over with."

Firestone brought over the tin container and the black rubber glove and stood there watching as Boneman picked up the glove, then discarded it, and then opened up the container, scooping a handful of white grease into his right hand. He then slathered it liberally over his hand before he aimed for the sergeant's hole. He dispensed with pleasantries and decided to begin with two fingers, and the sergeant grunted for the first time, acknowledging the intrusion.

"What do you want me to do?" Firestone asked dumbly.

"How about you keep him quiet."

"How?"

"Stick that thick cock of yours in his mouth … that should shut him up," Boneman suggested.

Firestone then positioned himself at Masters' head and grabbed his face, opened the older man's mouth and stuffed his stiff rod clear down to the hilt. He then fucked the sergeant's face with long, slow strokes, enjoying the warm feeling.

"Careful he doesn't bite the head off. If he tries, just punch him in the face," Boneman told his buddy.

Boneman then inserted a third finger, and Masters' dick twitched, and his groan was muffled, but he didn't clamp down on the thick meat he was sucking. Firestone kept up his rhythm as Boneman inserted another finger, making it four total. Again, Masters groaned, and Firestone's eyes rolled up. Boneman noticed Firestone's expression and barked, "Don't come yet, dumb ass, I'm just getting started."

Boneman rolled his four fingers around, loosening up the muscular hole, and slowly introduced his thumb. With that, Masters muffled a scream or was it a yell, and with Firestone's cock now resting in his mouth rather than pumping as he was trying to hold off, one couldn't tell. But, Boneman was not done. He then slowly worked his fist into the ass of his former drill instructor, and with a slow but steady motion, worked it all the way in, past his wrist and almost halfway up his forearm. Boneman's cock released a long stream of pre-cum that dangled to the floor; Firestone's eyes lit up at the sight of his buddy's arm up Masters' asshole; and Masters' eyes rolled up as his dick started to swell then twitch rapidly.

Firestone lost it first as the sight before him and the mouth on his hot cock was too much for the horny little muscleman. His cock shot a hefty load into the sergeant's mouth that the older man eagerly swallowed without missing a drop. And, that was enough to send Masters over the edge as the fist up his ass, the clothespins on his nipples, and the sweet load in his mouth made his eleven-inch cock twitch violently until he came clear up to his neck without even touching himself.

There was a lot of panting as Firestone removed his cock from Masters' mouth, and Boneman was the only one who still had full balls.

"Damn, did I give anyone permission to come!" Boneman yelled.

"Fuck you, prick," Masters said.

With that Boneman removed his fist from the sergeant's ass, walked over to the side of the sling, and punched him repeatedly in the stomach, which wasn't easy considering Masters was still in a supine position. Again, the rock hard abs against his fist turned Boneman on, and as he felt the load work its way out of his balls and up the length of his cock, he grabbed it and aimed for Masters' face, releasing a load that was heftier than the two released by the other men.

"Now, who's the prick, motherfucker?" Boneman said as he shook the last of his spunk out of his still-raging cock and onto the older man's mouth.

Masters just looked at him and smiled. Boneman let out a little grin also, and Firestone couldn't control himself any longer, saying, "Fuck, that was hot."

"Damn, if you don't stop breaking scene, Firestone, I am gonna stick my whole foot up your ass!" Boneman said, almost seriously.

"Promise?" Firestone asked with a smile.

# # # # #

After cleaning up, the three men were sitting in Masters' living room drinking a few beers and finishing one of the three pizzas they ordered. They were all wearing nothing but their boxers, and the pizza delivery guy had given them a curious look, but seeing the muscles on the three men, decided not to say anything, just collect his money and leave.

"So, how long to retirement?" Boneman asked.

"Four weeks," Masters answered as he took a swig of his beer.

"We'll be in Afghanistan by then," Firestone said with a sorrowful look.

Masters looked at the two young men he had trained not too long ago, and he felt a heaviness in his heart at the thought of them going off to war, but he was not one to get sentimental, at least not outwardly. He also silently prayed they would be OK and be able to see him again when they returned.

"Man have I got to take a piss," Masters announced as he stood up.

Firestone looked at him, then at Boneman, and got up from the couch and walked to the bathroom. Masters followed him, and Boneman did the same. When they arrived in the bathroom, Firestone was in the tub, naked and leaning on the wall.

Without saying a word, Masters dropped his boxers, whipped out his monster meat and aimed for the little muscleman, covering him with his hot stream. Boneman, positioned himself beside the sergeant, dropped his own boxers, put his arm around Masters' waist and added to Firestone's golden shower. Boneman then looked up at the sergeant, who then looked down at him and planted his mouth on the young jarhead's, driving his tongue inside and enjoying the taste of beer and pizza while they continued spraying their buddy, who by now was stroking his cock at the sight before him and the feeling of warm piss all over him.

WHO'S THE DADDY?
By Eric Summers

Wayne left work his usual time and drove home not thinking about much of anything. Lately, he had been in a funk. He didn't know why. His career was going great. He was in a happy loving relationship with a hot man twenty years his junior, and although he was fifty-five years old, he had the body of a man in his twenties. Wayne was over six-feet tall with two-hundred pounds of silver-fur covered muscle and a tight bubble-butt that would be the envy and desire of any man at any age. But, even with all he had going for him, he sighed as he pulled into the driveway.

He opened the front door and looked down to see his thirty-five-year-old partner, Marty, on all fours in the living room wearing nothing but a dog collar, a leash and a leather cock ring. Wayne looked at him and gave a faint smile. Normally, he would be up for some puppy play, but he couldn't muster the energy to train his dog today.

Wayne walked past the living room into the kitchen and opened the refrigerator. Marty stood up and followed him. Marty was four inches taller and had twenty-five more pounds of muscle than Wayne, and the cock ring only added to the allure of his long, thick cock and heavy balls. He had dark features and close-cropped black hair, and his body was smooth with just a touch of black hair in between his mountainous pecs that trailed down to his thick black pubic hair. He kept his huge balls shaved smooth, and Wayne kept Marty's crack shaved smooth as well, for he preferred it that way.

"Don't you want to play with me?" Marty asked as he licked Wayne's neck.

Wayne shrugged away. "I'm sorry, Babe, another time. I'm just not in the mood right now." He closed the refrigerator door after grabbing a beer, looked at Marty and grabbed the younger man's balls. "It's not you. It could never be you."

Marty's cock responded as it always did to Wayne's touch, but he knew that this was not the time to push his partner – or beg. Wayne released his balls and turned to look out the kitchen window while drinking his beer.

They had been together for twelve years, and each knew the other better than the back of his own hand. They knew when the other was not in the mood, and neither would push or whine just to play, probably because they played almost all the time and rarely were not in the mood. And, play they did – from puppy play to water sports, fisting, light bondage, heavy bondage, ball torture – you name it. But, no matter how they played, Wayne was always the dominant one, and Marty the submissive, and they took to their roles with relish.

Marty turned from the kitchen and went upstairs to change. A less secure partner would be hurt by the rejection, but Marty knew Wayne was in a funk. The problem was this funk seemed to last longer than usual as they had not played in more than a week – an eternity for them. He went into the bedroom, took off the collar and cock ring and put on a pair of sweatpants. Wayne entered the bedroom as Marty was tying the drawstring. He walked up to him, put his hand on the back of his head and kissed him long and hard. Again, Marty's cock responded. Wayne released his lips from Marty and looked down at the hefty bulge.

"God, you're a sexy motherfucker," he said to Marty with a smile.

Marty smiled back at him and said, "Why don't you go out tonight? Maybe you need to get some fresh air. I'll be all right. I have some more work to do anyway." Marty was a writer of gay erotica, and he worked from home and often into the night, so it was not unusual for him to suggest Wayne go out on his own.

"You sure?"

"Yeah … besides you seem a little distracted lately. Why don't you go to The Falcon. I hear the fleet is in town," Marty said with a grin.

Wayne agreed. He stripped off his business clothes, and although it had been more than a decade, Marty still got a thrill looking at his silver-fur covered muscular lover as he walked to the shower. He thought about joining him but decided it was best to leave Wayne alone.

Within an hour, Wayne was on his way to The Falcon, and Marty was tapping away at his computer.

The Falcon was the town's oldest leather bar, and on some nights, Wayne and Marty could swear there were still patrons there from opening night. However, The Falcon's location was advantageous as it was located near the Norfolk Naval Station, and when the fleet was in, it was hopping with hunky sailors looking for a good time.

Upon Marty's suggestion, Wayne dressed low key this evening and was wearing jeans, a black leather belt, a black T-shirt, and black motorcycle boots. He also decided to go commando, but that didn't stop him from putting on a leather studded cock-ring that Marty had recently bought for him. He entered The Falcon, nodded at a few familiar faces and seated himself at the bar. No sooner had he ordered a beer, when a hunky blond, who was obviously a sailor, sat next to him. Having served in the Navy, Wayne could spot a sailor from a mile away. Marty had also served in the Navy and was still a sailor when he met Wayne.

"What's your rate?" Wayne asked knowing that the word "rank" did not apply to Navy enlisted men.

"Senior Chief Petty Officer," the blond responded in an equally hunky voice. "You must have served."

"Twenty years ... Master Chief Petty Officer," Wayne responded.

"I guess that makes you the Daddy," the hunk said as he swigged his beer.

Wayne smiled but did not respond.

"So, Master Chief Petty Officer, what are you looking for tonight?"

Wayne took a good long look at the hunk. He was thickly muscled, not unlike Marty, but with piercing blue eyes rather than

Marty's black eyes. He had to be no older than thirty. But, Wayne preferred black men like Marty.

"What's your name, sailor?"

"Adam, and yours, Daddy?"

"Wayne," he told him while his eyes trailed down to the large basket that strained the crotch of his jeans. Adam was wearing a white T-shirt that hid little of his physique, and Wayne liked what he saw, but again, he just wasn't in the mood. "I have a partner ... we have an understanding ... but I'm just not in the mood to play Daddy tonight ... I hope you understand."

Adam looked right at Wayne, put his hand on Wayne's crotch and said, "Good. Because I'm not in the mood to play boy." He gave Wayne a squeeze, released him and looked up at the TV screen, which was showing some reality nonsense no one cared to watch.

Wayne took a swig of his beer, and suddenly, he was intrigued. He had never played submissive. He never had to. His hair had gone prematurely gray, and for as long as he was into the scene, he gladly played the Daddy. Being with Marty was easy because as big as Marty was, he loved being the submissive. This was a huge turn-on when they first met as Wayne never dated anyone taller than he, especially someone who was also more muscular, and finding a muscle boy who enjoyed taking orders was a treat indeed. They were also madly in love with each other, but they always had an understanding. They knew men were pigs and monogamy was near impossible. The only rule was they had to give total disclosure – and all the details. Marty loved hearing the details, often including them in his writing or just jacking off while listening to Wayne recount his escapades.

Funny thing was Wayne, who was twenty years older, played way more than Marty did. He once questioned him about this, feeling guilty for always engaging in extracurricular activities. Marty said that as a submissive he oftentimes found it hard to trust people, so he preferred to be careful as the scenes he enjoyed opened someone up to serious danger if one got carried away. He also assured Wayne that he was totally cool with Wayne playing around, joking that he only had a few good years left. Wayne ended up taking Marty over his knee and spanking him for that comment and ended up with his muscle boy's spunk all over his leg as a result. Then Wayne handcuffed Marty and fucked him doggy-style on the floor as punishment for not feeding his spunk to his Daddy. Marty was sure to let Wayne know when he was about to blow, and Wayne flipped him over and slapped Marty's balls while swallowing his load, and his boy was in heaven.

Wayne looked over at Adam and thought about the proposition. He could not remember the last time someone offered to dominate him. Did anyone ever offer? He thought back but could not recall.

"You got a place?" Wayne asked, surprised at his quickness to respond.

"I got a friend with a basement set-up ... you interested?" Adam said, looking over at Wayne.

Wayne finished his beer, set the bottle on the bar, spun to face Adam and said, "If you got the balls, yeah, I'm interested."

Adam gulped down the rest of his beer, got up from his stool and headed out the bar.

Once outside, he grabbed Wayne's ass and said, "My friend's place is a short drive, you got a car?"

Wayne agreed to drive, and they drove over to Granby Street to his friend's house. Upon pulling into the driveway, Wayne started to get a little nervous. He thought about how Marty said he needed to be careful as a submissive and not all guys could be trusted. Although Adam was a bit shorter than Wayne, he was packed with muscle.

"Listen, I'm not sure ..." Wayne began.

"Hey, I know," Adam interrupted. "Look, I'm not out to hurt you, just have a good time. We'll even set some ground rules if you like."

"OK," Wayne answered. "No bareback, no blood, no scat, and no drugs."

"That's cool. I gotta stay safe if I want to keep my job."

"Nothing that will leave a mark, or at least a permanent one, as I have to go to work on Monday," Wayne said with a smile.

"Totally cool," Adam agreed. He then exited the car, and Wayne did the same.

Wayne stopped Adam before they reached the door, grabbed his arm and said, "And, I don't bottom. I don't get fisted and nothing gets shoved up there."

Adam looked at Wayne's ass and shook his head, "Too bad ... but I guess that's cool, too."

They entered the house, and Adam took off his shirt right after closing the front door. Wayne took a look at Adam's body, and his breath was taken away. The Senior Chief Petty Officer had the body of a god, covered in light blond hair, and he thought that this guy would be perfect for Marty, who liked that type. He reached over to grab a pec, but Adam grabbed his wrist and said, "I didn't say you could touch me."

"Yes, Sir," Wayne answered as he followed him into the kitchen.

"You want something to drink?"

Thinking he better keep his wits about him, Wayne asked for water. Adam pulled two bottles of water out of the fridge and handed one to Wayne.

"My friend is out to sea, so he said I could use his place whenever I am in town and on leave," he told Wayne.

He then put his bottle down and reached for Wayne's shirt. Wayne didn't resist as Adam pulled his shirt over his head. He obviously liked what he saw and roughly felt Wayne's muscles. He then reached for Wayne's belt, but stopped.

"Take off your boots, boy."

Wayne did as he was ordered.

"Now the jeans."

Wayne again obeyed. He was now naked except for the leather studded cock-ring, and his dick was getting hard and almost to its full thick nine inches. Adam grabbed his dick and said, "Nothing like a boy with a big dick … you need to piss?"

"Yes, Sir."

"The bathroom's right over there," Adam said as he pointed across the hall. "Leave the door open."

Wayne did as he was told. His dick went down slightly as he started to piss, and just as his stream started, Adam walked in and watched him piss. Wayne looked over, and Adam was now naked with the exception of a brass cock-ring that encased one of the thickest cocks he had ever seen. Wayne figured hard it was probably seven inches and at least seven or even eight around also. Wayne finished pissing and shook his cock, and as he went to step out, Adam stopped him.

"Grab mine, I gotta go."

Wayne wrapped his hand around the Senior Chief Petty Officer's cock and pointed it at the bowl. Adam let go with a strong stream of piss that would make a garden hose jealous, and the feeling of holding that thick rod while it drained caused Wayne's cock to rise up to full attention. When Adam was done, he shook his cock for him, and it started getting hard from the attention.

"Don't move," Adam said as he exited the bathroom.

He returned seconds later with a collar and a leash. He snapped the collar around Wayne's neck and led him out of the bathroom down the hall and downstairs to the basement.

The basement was not the dungeon Wayne expected. There was a bed, a dresser and not much else. It was dimly lit and smelled a bit musty. Adam led Wayne over to the bed and ordered him to lie down on his back. He then took the leash and secured it to the wall on a hook behind the bed. Adam then reached under the bed and grabbed a rubber restraint and secured Wayne's left wrist, walked around and did the same with the right wrist. Adam admired the sight before him then secured Wayne's ankles the same way he secured his wrists.

Wayne was alternating between being turned on and being nervous. Adam sensed this and walked over to the head of the bed, bent down and kissed Wayne hard on the mouth wrestling his tongue with Wayne's.

"Don't worry, boy. Daddy's gonna take good care of you," he said as he released his mouth then he ran his fingers through Wayne's hair.

Wayne's dick started to get hard again as he watched Adam walk over to the dresser and admired how the sailor's muscular butt flexed as he bent down to open the bottom drawer.

Adam turned around holding two nipple clamps and a candle. He walked over to Wayne and scanned his body before putting the nipple clamps on him. Wayne moaned when the clamps were applied, and his cock let out a stream of pre-cum, which did not go unnoticed.

"Whatta ya know, you little pig, leaking like a faucet," Adam said with a smile.

Adam then located a lighter on the dresser and lit the candle. He walked over to Wayne holding the lit candle about twelve inches above Wayne's chest. Wayne felt assured at that moment because an expert knew to hold the candle to allow the wax to cool a bit on its way down and not leave a scar. For the first time, Wayne truly relaxed in Adam's presence.

Wayne flinched when the first drop landed on his chest, and his dick twitched and leaked some more. Adam worked the wax down his torso, and with each drop, Wayne leaked. By the time, Adam reached his balls (he skipped his dick), there was enough pre-cum to fill a bucket. Wayne was in ecstasy as his nipples were pinched hard by the clamps and the hot wax landed on his big smooth balls. He also knew that if Adam kept that up, he was going to come, and somehow Adam also sensed this. He stopped dripping wax on Wayne and blew out the candle.

Adam walked back over to the bed and twisted one of the nipple clamps causing Wayne to half moan, half scream, then he squeezed the other one getting the same reaction. Without saying a word, Adam climbed on top of Wayne and straddled his face, facing away from him, dropping his huge nuts toward his mouth and his ass toward his nose.

"Lick my balls, boy."

Wayne went to town on those furry balls. He slathered them and rolled them in his mouth and tried to get both in his mouth at once. This was not easy considering he was restrained and collared. Adam's muscular legs did a good job of holding him up, so he did not crush Wayne's face, but this was not easy as Wayne was an oral expert, and Adam's cock was leaking almost as much as Wayne's. Adam then scooted forward.

"Lick my hot hole, boy."

And, Wayne did as he was told. He did his best to get his tongue between those muscular cheeks and licked the blond fur-covered hole, almost coming just from the feeling of having this muscle hunk squatting over his face.

Adam never experienced anything like Wayne's technique, and the sight of Wayne's huge leaking cock was making him want more. He let Wayne get him really wet then he hopped off the bed.

"Good boy."

Wayne's tongue was sore, but in a good way.

Adam walked over to the dresser again and opened the top drawer and pulled out a bottle of Gun Oil, a packet of condoms and a ball gag.

Wayne started to protest, but Adam was quick to place the ball gag over his mouth. Now, Wayne was starting to get scared again, but Adam leaned down, ran his fingers through his hair and said, "Relax, boy. I know the rules." Then he grabbed Wayne's still raging dick. "And you better not lose this hard-on, boy."

Adam opened the condom packet with his teeth and rolled it onto Wayne's dick. He then pumped some of the Gun Oil into his palm, rubbed some on Wayne's cock and then lubed his ass with his own fingers.

"Now, boy, if you fuck Daddy really good, I'll have a nice treat for you."

Adam again straddled Wayne, but facing him this time, and with one fell swoop impaled himself on Wayne's thick nine inches. He then grabbed the nipple clamps and rode that hard cock while twisting on those clamps. Wayne bucked up as best he could while the blond muscle hunk sailor gave his own quads a good workout riding him up and down. Adam's thick cock grew even thicker with each thrust, and the head was swollen and purple and smacking against his belly. Wayne felt his own cock growing in length as he felt sensations he had not felt in a long time.

"Come on, boy, fuck me good!" Adam ordered.

With the ball gag, he was finding it hard to respond, but his eyes said it all.

Adam stopped twisting the clamps and flexed his biceps for Wayne and licked them admiring himself in the process while continuing to squat up and down on the large cock that impaled his hot hole. He then ran his hands over his pecs and gave Wayne quite a muscle show, flexing and feeling and licking himself.

How does he know how much flexing turns me on? Wayne thought. If he doesn't stop, I'm going to shoot!

Adam continued to flex and squat until his dick was so hard it hurt. He reached down while still riding Wayne and removed the ball gag. Then, he pulled off Wayne's dick, moved forward and shoved his aching cock into Wayne's mouth, and his extra-thick cock shot a huge load into his mouth and down his throat. Wayne swallowed every delicious drop. All this action was too much for him, and he shot a huge load of his own into the condom that was still on his dick.

Adam stepped off the bed and looked down at the cum-filled rubber, and out of breath, but laughing, he said, "You fucking cum pig."

Wayne said nothing as he tried to catch his breath and continued to taste the semen from the sailor.

Adam then undid the restraints and the collar, and Wayne thanked him.

"You may wanna shower before you go home," Adam said.

Wayne took him up on his offer and once cleaned up and dressed was ready to leave, totally satisfied.

"Thank you, Sir. That was just what I needed," Wayne said as he shook Adam's hand.

"Well, it is what Marty said you wanted," Adam said with a wink.

"That little shit," Wayne responded shaking his head.

"Hey he ain't so little, and be nice to him. There aren't too many partners who would do what he did for you," Adam admonished.

Wayne knew Adam was right and knew at that moment he loved Marty more than anything.

"Tell me then. Did you ever bottom for Marty?" Wayne asked.

"With a cock like his? Of course. Don't you?" Adam asked as if the answer were obvious.

Wayne didn't answer. He gave Adam his number and suggested a three-way sometime, which Adam eagerly agreed would be fun.

Wayne arrived home an hour later to find Marty had already gone to bed. He stripped off his clothes and crawled into bed with his lover. Marty moaned as Wayne spooned him and grabbed his Daddy's hand, pulling it to his chest.

"Did you have a good time, Daddy?" he asked sleepily.

"If you fuck me, boy, I'll tell you all about it," Wayne growled.

Marty's eyes popped open, for he wasn't sure he heard what he thought he heard.

Wayne then pulled Marty on top of him, wrapped his legs around his boy's waist and begged him to drive his huge cock into him.

Marty immediately grabbed some lube from the nightstand, greased up Wayne's asshole and rammed his huge hard cock all the way into his Daddy before he changed his mind.

In ten years, he had never fucked Wayne, and he was not about to miss this opportunity. Wayne didn't protest Marty's rough treatment and no-holds-barred fucking, actually getting totally turned on and rock-hard from the way his boy wasted no time impaling him. Marty leaned in and kissed him roughly and told him how much he loved him, while Wayne reciprocated, and Marty gave his Daddy the ride of a lifetime, practically fucking him into the next building. Wayne loved every minute of it as his muscle boy pounded his virgin hole with all his super strength, feeling those huge balls slap against his ass while Marty's muscular body glistened with sweat from the workout.

It was a total muscle fuck.

And, all the neighbors heard for hours that night was "Fuck me, boy! Come on, you can fuck Daddy harder than that!" along with the grunts and heavy breathing of a muscle boy giving his Daddy the ride of a lifetime.

Anchors aweigh!

THE WINDOW ESTIMATE
By Eric Summers

I hate being an apartment manager, and I only agreed to do it because my landlords promised me a fifty percent reduction in the rent for the four years they would be in Brazil. The worst part is that I have to listen to the constant complaining from the fat redneck, her drunk asshole of a husband and her future serial killer, slut daughter upstairs. I just wish the daughter would get it over with and kill them already, so I can clean up the mess and rent the place out to a couple of hotties. But, until then, I have to be the responsible one and that includes getting estimates for work that I would rather let go in the hopes the cast from *Cops* upstairs will leave in frustration.

Most of the time, these estimates are for things they have broken, and I know that the constant yelling and banging that goes on is the reason the frame of the large bay window in their master bedroom was cracked causing the glass to fall down into the wall, leaving a four-inch gap on the top.

I took my sweet time getting an estimate, but when the rain seeped in causing water to leak into my apartment, it became my personal problem, so I called a couple of window companies. I figured I would punish the landlords as well for sticking me with these assholes and get an estimate for all the windows.

Two salesmen had been here already, but they were so slick, I threw away their estimates before the door closed behind them.

On the day the third and final guy was to arrive, I pretty much didn't care anymore. I decided to work from home that day, so it was amazing I even bothered to shower, although I only wore a pair of gym shorts (actually cut-off sweat pants) and a wife-beater. I was totally engrossed in work when I heard a knock at the door.

I opened the door and standing there was what looked to be a teenager, wearing a loose fitting All-Weather Window Company polo shirt. He gave me the taillights to headlights three-second once over I tend to get from guys who see me for the first time, which doesn't even faze me anymore.

You see, I am an ex-professional football player (not that anyone remembers – third string tackle), and I am six-foot even, weighing in at around two-hundred-sixty pounds. Just a big black hulking dude. At thirty-five, I still work out as if I am being paid to, and I won't deny I ever took a needle in the ass. We'll leave it at that. Now, I work as a bookkeeper for a nondescript company in a nondescript cubicle located in a nondescript building. I am one of the lucky few to have actually gotten paid to be a professional football player, but after almost five years on the bench, I got bored. I was told I was too nice, not aggressive enough, but the coach liked me, so I held onto my job.

Now, the kid in front of me may have played some sports. He had that college jock, too many frat parties body. You know the type – broad shoulders, decent arms, and remnants of the freshman forty still around the middle. If they are straight, the paunch is there for life, and if they are gay, well, they wouldn't have taken on the freshman-forty in the first place. No gay boy in his twenties would allow such a thing to happen to him. This kid was definitely straight, which was fine with me as I don't like them young. I like them older, much older. I like being fucked silly by a big muscle bear with gray hair. If this kid had a twelve-inch dick, I couldn't have cared less.

"Mr. Kennedy?"

I let him in, and he introduced himself as Allan. I showed him all the windows upstairs and downstairs in all the apartments. Of course, the redneck had to butt in and say what she wanted in a window, but I shut her up immediately and continued to follow Allan from wall to wall while he measured and wrote on his legal pad.

When we were done, we returned to my apartment, and I had to ask him his age.

"I'm twenty-three. I couldn't find a job in my field, so I took this sales job, which has made my college education a waste ... can I ask you a question, a personal question?"

I said sure.

"I can see you work out …"

He could see I work out. He was brilliant. My arms relaxed are eighteen inches around. My pecs are so huge, I can't see my feet, and he can see I work out.

"I've been trying to lose this gut since I graduated, and nothing I do works. Should I do more cardio?"

"You should quit drinking so much beer," I said and raised my eyebrows. I may let a quack doc shoot what is probably horse piss into my ass to get huge and ripped, but I never drank or did drugs. Yeah, I know, what I do is just as bad. Whatever. You'd fuck me if you had a chance, especially if you saw my rock hard and huge bubble-butt.

"Yeah, I guess you're right."

"So, how long before I get an estimate?" I asked.

"Oh, I can have one for you this afternoon. I'll email it to you."

And with that, he was gone.

I went back to work and took a mid-day break to go to the gym because I have body dysmorphia or manorexia or some other psychological shit because I think I'm fat or skinny and have deep emotional issues. Please. I know what I look like. I look like a fucking freak, but I like the freak look, and the old muscle bear dads I let fuck me like it, too. Don't assume you know guys like me.

After I returned from the gym, I was mixing myself a protein shake when there was a knock at the door. I was back in my cut-off sweat shorts but not wearing a shirt anymore. I opened the door, and it was frat-boy window guy.

"I decided to hand deliver the estimate," he said as he handed me the envelope. "I can explain it to you if you like?"

I gave him my best you think I am a dunder-headed muscle boy with the IQ of a baboon look.

"Oh, I didn't mean it like that … uh, I mean I like to explain why we may be higher than most anyone else," Allan recovered.

"I may look mean, but it takes a whole hell of a lot to offend me or piss me off … believe me, kid, I haven't lost my temper in years," I said with a smile as I motioned him inside.

What, you say? A juiced-up freak who hasn't had a roid induced hissy fit? See, you read too much. I have never been a hot head. That is why I sucked as a professional football player. I'm too easy going. The only side effect I ever got from the juice was shrunken balls, but I can still come a gallon of spunk – it's just clear.

I offered Allan a protein shake, and he accepted. As we sat there drinking our whey concoctions, he explained all the window crap, and I pretended to listen, but I couldn't get over how he was avoiding looking at me. I was shirtless, pumped from the gym and sitting no more than two feet away from him. Although I had showered at the gym, I hadn't bothered putting on deodorant, so I had a light musk about me, which some guys like.

When he finally looked up, I could tell he was enthralled by my pumped pecs and my nipples, which I pulled on constantly. They stick out a good inch even now.

"You want to touch them?" I asked.

His eyes bulged.

"Look, it won't make you gay. Straight guys always want to touch my muscles to see what they feel like. Are they hard, soft, will they vibrate?" I said with a chuckle and a smile.

"Sure," he said as he slowly reached over to kind of poke a finger at my bicep.

I flexed it for him, and he then caressed it a bit before taking his hand away. So, I was wrong about him. He was a big ole fag. I grabbed his hand and put it on my pec while I made it bounce.

"Damn, they are hard as a rock," he said.

I was not turned on by this. He just wasn't my type. Yeah, I know, get over it.

"Now, about this estimate. What can we do to get you to come down by at least ten percent?" I may have been pissed at the landlords, but I was still a tightwad at heart, and I wasn't going for the obvious scene you are expecting here.

"Become my personal trainer," he said.

I sat back and looked at him. He had potential and a good frame. And that gut he complained about wasn't really that bad, just a little soft.

"Take off your shirt," I said.

He stood up and without hesitation removed his shirt. His shoulders were broad, and his biceps a nice size, too. However, his chest was a surprise as it was huge, which made me make a mental note to suggest he wear a tighter company shirt, and it was covered with hair, curly blond hair that trailed down to his pants.

"You'll have to shave that," I said pointing to his chest.

"Really?" he said as he ran his hand seductively down his torso.

"But not until after you bend me over this table and fuck my brains out. The condoms and lube are in the drawer behind you. If you want me to train you, you better be ready to do what I say at the drop of a hat," I said without stopping to take a breath. Then I stood, dropped my cut-off sweat shorts revealing my hard six-inch dick. Yeah, I know, everyone in these stories is hung like a horse, especially the black guys like me. Well, I'm a bottom, and I may not have a lot of dick to play with, but I certainly have enough muscle to make up for it. Besides, little dicks get hard, stay hard, and shoot nice big loads. So, get over it.

I also know that I said he wasn't my type. But, I wanted that estimate lowered, and my hole filled at the same time. He was there; I was horny; do the math.

I then bent over the table, while he fumbled around with his pants.

"Hurry up, I don't get this horny often, just grease it up and plug me," I said over my shoulder.

I then felt the cold lube dribbling down my crack. He sort of rubbed it all around, and I could tell he was nervous. I then heard the condom wrapper being opened; he cursed himself while he tried to roll it on. I clearly had him flustered.

"Are these the largest ones you have?" he asked.

I turned around and saw what looked to be a good ten thick inches of circumcised dick sticking straight out at me. There you go – a horse-hung top in a porno story. Are you happy now?

"Look in the back of the drawer. They must have slid back. There should be some extra-hungs or whatever they call them," I said as I marveled at his heat-seeking moisture missile, which is a friend's nickname for huge cocks.

"Found them," he said with delight.

"Good, slip one on and fuck my brains out," I said as I again bent over the table. "And, don't bother eating me out or fingering me, just stick that barbell up my chute ... I hate foreplay."

He did just that. All the way in, no apologies, no hesitation, no finesse, no bullshit, and I loved it.

"Now, reach around and pull my nipples as hard as you can while you fuck me."

And, he did just that. He reached around and pulled my big nipples, no apologies, no hesitation, no finesse, no bullshit, and I loved it.

He practically pounded my huge muscular ass over the moon (excuse the pun) and pulled my nipples another inch. I was in heaven. He was having a pretty good time, too. Or, he was good at faking it because he kept telling me what a hot ass I had and what a sexy motherfucker I was. And at one point, he started nibbling on the back of my neck, and that did it.

I cried out as I came. I wasn't even touching myself since I was using my hands to hold onto the edge of the table while he pounded me for points. And, right after I came, he filled that extra large rubber with his own load and yelled out loud what a "man slut" I was, and amazingly, I came again – hands free.

When he recovered, he apologized for calling me a man slut and gave me ten percent off on the windows in addition to another ten percent for the hot fuck.

I never told him, but calling me a man slut was the best part of the fuck.

The windows look great. And Allan? He is a muscle freak now, too.

I love being me.

Connor Maguire

#oneclickaway